英文秘道
踏上學習英文的成功路

OXFORD
UNIVERSITY PRESS
牛津大學出版社

OXFORD
UNIVERSITY PRESS

Oxford University Press is a department of the University of Oxford.
It furthers the University's objective of excellence in research, scholarship,
and education by publishing worldwide. Oxford is a registered trade mark of
Oxford University Press in the UK and in certain other countries

Published in Hong Kong by
Oxford University Press (China) Limited
18th Floor, Warwick House East, Taikoo Place, 979 King's Road, Quarry Bay,
Hong Kong

3 5 7 9 10 8 6 4 2

ISBN: 978-0-19-941628-8

目錄

作者序

香港人對英語文法掌握得好嗎？如果問問大學教授或職場的上司，恐怕他們都苦笑。一般人縱使學了十多年英文，仍然把 please reply (to me) 說成 Please reply；把 Let me do it 說成 Let me to do it；更不要說懂得何時用 will、何時用 would，和為甚麼 look forward to 後面要用動詞的 -ing 形式。

問題究竟出在哪裏？我曾當前線英語教師十五年，從事英語教師培訓二十多年，觀過的英文課超過二千，看到的情況，就是雖然老師們都鍥而不捨的解釋各個文法規條，指正學生們作文中層出不窮的錯誤，而學生由小一開始已經日復一日的做文法練習，但是我們的英語教學中卻偏偏欠缺了一個重要環節，就是語言覺識 (language awareness) 的訓練。

試觀察身邊的英文達人，除了努力，他們都有一個共同點，就是對語文有很高的敏感度，無論是聽到一個字的不同發音，在街上看見一個路牌的特別寫法，或閱報時看到一個單字的另類意思，他們都立刻注意到；就是這對語言的敏感度，幫助他們學到不少課堂沒有教的語言特質，從而對語言有更成熟的掌握。我的工作是訓練英語教師，但我常對人打趣的說，要學好英文，如果單單依靠老師，你的英文也許不錯，但不會很超卓。

語言覺識的重要，還可以從以下的情景看出來：對於有意學好英文的人，我們都會建議他們多聽多讀，但有經驗的英語教師都會知道，一些學生的確可以從多聽多讀中得益，但同時有不少學生，無論多努力多聽多

讀，英文都沒有甚麼大進步；這中間的分野，就是語言覺識高低之分別。

在學術界，語言覺識這概念存在已久，不同學者有略為不同的定義，我覺得英國學者 Ronald Carter 的定義最易瞭解：'an enhanced consciousness of and sensitivity to the forms and functions of language (2003, p. 64)'，（對語言的形式和功能的高度意識和敏感度）。當然，語言覺識並不單對文法的敏感度，它還包括對語言各環節的感知，例如音韻 (phonology)、話語 (discourse)、語義 (semantics) 和體裁 (genre)。作家林沛理在《EQ 英文智商》一書中，則列舉了語言智慧中的五大元素。但到目前為止，語言覺識這概念應用於文法教學上最有成效。

為甚麼語言覺識的訓練這麼重要？首先，無論學校的教學，還是坊間的文法參考書，為了幫助學生和讀者的理解，都會傾向把文法歸納成簡單的規則，例如現在式 (present tense) 就是描述現在的事情，過去式 (past tense) 就是描述過去的事情，但英文的時態的實際運用，千變萬化，單靠依從簡單化了的規條，實不能攀上更高的語文境界。

再者，學校的文法教學，和坊間的文法練習，都會傾向注重語言的形式 (language form)，多於語言的功能 (language function)，例如處理語態 (voice) 時，會給予學生大量把句子從主動語態 (active voice) 轉換為被動語態 (passive voice) 的訓練，而少有訓練學生判斷在不同的語境下，兩個語態應如何取捨；這傾向和教育評核一般只著重學生獲得正確答案有關。

此外，每種成熟的語言，都擁有不少細緻或含蓄的表達方法，這些細微的分別，往往只能意會，而不能依靠機械的文法規條去分析，例如 I hope you will come to my wedding 和 I'm hoping you will come to my wedding，如果要用說話解釋兩者之分別，恐怕只會愈說愈亂。又例如，為何 I don't think you've got the right answer，比 I think you haven't got the right answer 聽起來較自然，也需要有高水平的語言覺識，才能領悟其中的分別。

從學習心理學角度，恐怕沒有多少人會很狂熱的學習文法規條，或很享受機械式的文法練習。語言覺識訓練，給予學習者特別設計的語料 (language data)，然後邀請學習者就語料進行各式把玩，例如分類、重組、排序、判斷，這過程充滿認知挑戰 (cognitive challenge)，這正正迎合了多數現代人的學習心理，而這積極的思考過程，亦加深了對學習內容的記憶。

本書通過五十個實例，去提高讀者的語言覺識，讀者固然可以加深對這五十個文法難題的認識，但是本書更重要的目的，是加深讀者對學習文法的興趣，和文法是甚麼的瞭解，從而提高讀者的語言敏感度。最後一提的，是書中採用的語料，其中部分可能不為傳統文法所接受，或具爭議性，但這亦正好反映了語言覺識的重要。

施敏文

Foreword by Dr Icy Lee

Although language awareness is an established area of language acquisition research and is pivotal to the development of second language competence, it is under-emphasized in the local language classroom. Traditionally English teachers busy themselves with grammar teaching that primarily takes the form of grammar drilling, reducing grammar to a set of rules and rendering it an end rather than a means to an end. Grammar is not simply about the memorization and regurgitation of rules; it is a vehicle for meaning making. With strong language awareness, students are able to understand how grammar is used to make meaning, and in turn they are able to make meaning appropriately with grammar. Thus, language awareness training should be an important part of grammar teaching.

To illustrate the usefulness of language awareness, we can compare the two expressions 'I love it' and 'I'm loving it' (used by McDonald's in its commercial campaign a few years back). Hong Kong students can easily tell the difference in the tenses used and may even be able to articulate the grammar rules associated with the two tenses. However, it is one thing to know that 'I love it' uses the simple present tense and 'I'm loving it' the present continuous tense, but quite another to understand the subtleties and nuances of meaning expressed by the less common expression 'I'm loving it' (because traditional grammar states that we don't usually use 'love' in the continuous tenses).

In this inspiring book, Dr Paul Sze exemplifies the notion of language awareness by drawing on examples from daily life. While the field of second language teaching has been rather slow in picking up and developing the notion of language awareness, this book fills the void by providing a useful resource for the readers to enhance their sensitivity to the interplay between grammar and communication, and for teachers to incorporate language awareness training into their own grammar lessons.

The notion of language awareness has been around for quite some time within the academia, but there is a paucity of resources which introduce the concept to a wider audience. This is a must-read book for those with a strong interest in effective language acquisition, particularly of grammar.

Dr Icy Lee（李潔冰）
Professor, Faculty of Education
The Chinese University of Hong Kong

（譯文）語言覺識在語言習得研究中，已是一個極受尊重的範圍，而且語言覺識對於第二語言能力的發展，起着關鍵性的作用，但是在本地的英語課程中，還沒有得到足夠的重視。一些教法傳統的教師仍然非常依賴機械化的文法操練，把文法簡化成純粹的規條，並把教授這些規條當為目的，而不是幫助學生學會溝通的手段。文法學習不應是死記硬背的語法規條，而是幫助我們表情達意的工具。學生如果有高水平的語言覺識，便能更有效和準確地表達意思，故此語言覺識是文法教學的重要部分。

要明白語言覺識的重要，我們可以嘗試比較 I love it 和 I'm loving it 這兩個說法（後者是某連鎖快餐店的宣傳語句）。香港學生都能夠指出兩個句子中動詞的時態，他們甚至可以清楚解釋兩個時態的分別。但是，知道 I love it 是簡單現在式，和 I'm loving it 是現在進行式，不代表學生能領悟較罕見的 I'm loving it 所表達的細緻的感覺。事實上，傳統文法甚至否定將動詞 love 在進行式中使用。

在《英文秘道》中，施敏文博士 (Dr Paul Sze) 利用一系列日常生活的英語實例，去闡述語言覺識這概念，在英語教學界對語言覺識仍相對陌生的背景下，本書提供了有用的學習資源，以幫助學生和一般讀者掌握文法和傳意的互動關係，教師亦可以之作為參考，嘗試將語言覺識引進其文法課之中。

語言覺識這概念已出現了一段日子，唯相關的教材卻鳳毛麟角，本書將這概念，通過實例推介給公眾，實至為珍貴。

梁賀琪博士序

近年常聽到語言覺識 (language awareness) 一詞，初時沒有特別為意，後來在好友施敏文博士 (Dr Paul Sze) 的社交網站帖文中經常看到這個詞。酷愛文字的他常圖文並茂把有趣的例子與大家分享，漸漸令我這個現時專注管理的前英文教師重拾對語文的興趣。有時雖然忙碌，但也禁不住在他的面書塗鴉牆上流連近三十分鐘，看看他的新帖與高質素的留言。Paul 細心的解說，每字每句都透露着他温文爾雅的性格卻又有掩不住的激情與力量，這種力量絕對足以感染其他的語言學習者。

有人覺得學英文但求溝通，文法錯無傷大雅；又有人覺得我們學中文也不多學文法，學英文也應該以「實用」為主。看過這本書，你會發現英文文法不是一些無聊死板的規條，亦不可與日常應用分割。有了對語言準確性的警覺能力，在每日的應用裏多加印證、比較與觀察，不難發現文法根本活在每字、每句、每個語境之中。

'No fouling' 與 'Do not foul' 作告示時有何分別；'volunteer parent' 與 'parent volunteer' 何者更為正確；為甚麼 'look forward to' 後必須用 'ing' 形式？這些問題都可以在此書中找到詳細易明的答案與解釋，而且趣味盎然。

看罷此書可能未必立即成為英語專家，但肯定你跟我一樣，會在不知不覺中提高了自己的語言覺識，和更能領悟學習語文的樂趣。

好好享受，高質素的書不多。

梁賀琪（June Leung）
資深教育工作者、遵理集團創辦人

林沛理序
—— 有效使用英文的神奇鎖匙

學英文也許沒有捷徑，卻肯定有一條通往其有效使用的秘道 (secret passage)，從事英語教師培訓工作多年的施敏文博士 (Dr. Paul Sze) 稱之為「語言覺識」。

語言覺識 (language awareness) 是語言學 (linguistics) 的重要概念，也是理解文學作品和文字創作的關鍵。甚麼是語言覺識？那是一種對語言的形式 (form)、效果 (effect)、巧妙 (subtlety) 和細膩 (nuances) 的在意、洞察和領悟。從蘇東坡的「回首向來瀟灑處，歸去，也無風雨也無晴」到相機的廣告標語 'I reach the end only because I dare to begin'，展現的都是不同程度、深淺和層次的語言覺識。

外國不少研究顯示，學生的語言觸覺與語言能力 (language competence) 有密切關係。觸覺敏銳的學生，聽說讀寫的能力往往勝人不止一籌。

很可惜，「語言觸覺」的重要性在香港的教育界沒有得到廣泛的認同。施敏文博士是本地少數致力推廣這個概念的英語教學專家。他認為沒有為學生提供足夠的語感訓練，是香港學校英語教學的一大缺失。他建議老師進行多些磨利觸覺和加強意識 (consciousness-raising) 的課堂活動，目的不是要訓練學生的考試技巧，又或者要他們在短時間內找到正確答案；而是要提高他們對英文的領悟力和敏感度。

他的新書《英文秘道》幫助讀者將表達方式道地、符合語言習慣的 'idiomatic English' 與想當然的港式英語

區分起來。最難能可貴的是，他從生活出發，以談佚事和說趣聞的方式 (anecdotal approach) 切入，舉重若輕。

　　英文重文法 (grammar)，中文重語感，這是多數人持有的觀點，已成語文學習的傳統智慧。《英文秘道》提醒我們，學好英文，除了要掌握文法還要發展語感。如果英文是勝景、福地和樂土，我們單走文法這條正路永遠到不了目的地，還要踏上語感這條秘道和幽徑，最後才會發現英文的奇偉壯麗，千嬌百媚。

林沛理

牛津大學出版社

英語教學出版總編輯

尋找 地道 的 英語

1 要地道還是要準確？

blood donor centre 和 blood donation centre 是不同的地方？

捐血站應該叫做 blood donor centre 還是 blood donation centre 呢？我循着指示牌的方向走去，看看究竟是捐血站還是供捐血者見面或活動的地方。結果就如告示牌的中文所示，那是供人捐血的地方。

既然那是供人捐血的地方，那麼英文的 blood donor centre 是否應該改作 blood donation centre 呢？這卻不是一個容易回答的問題。首先，從文法角度而言，blood donor centre 完全沒有問題；有些人可能會覺得 blood donor centre 不及中文的「捐血站」那麼直接準確，但 blood donor centre 卻是很地道 (idiomatic) 的英語，如果使用谷歌 (Google) 搜尋，你會發現 blood donor centre 比 blood donation centre 常用得多。

這個例子提醒我們，運用英文時除了要注意文法是否正確，說法是否地道也是考慮因素之一。請讀讀以下兩個例句，看看哪一句聽起來較為自然：

(1) I think he doesn't know the answer.

(2) I don't think he knows the answer.

上面兩個句子都合乎文法，意思大致相同，但除非有特殊的傳意需要，在大部分的情況下，以英語為母語的人士會說 (2) 而不說 (1)，即 (2) 的說法在一般情況下比 (1) 的說法更為地道。

口語英語更有地道與不夠地道之分。以下三段對話中，B 的回應大概都是學校正規英語課程所教授的：

A: 'How are you?'

B: 'I'm fine. Thank you.'

A: 'How about another beer?'

B: 'No, thanks.'

A: 'I hope you're not upset with that?'

B: 'Not really.'

然而，在現今英語世界裏，對於以上的三個情況，更地道的回答都可以是 I'm good。地道的說法在文法上不一定是最正確或最合理的，例如起初流行以 I'm good 回應 How are you? 時，一些學究氣（pedantic）的人便不以為然，覺得人家又不是問你是好人還是壞人，為甚麼要自詡 I'm good 呢？但是地道就是地道，你只能跟從或不跟從。

現今英語已成為國際語言，雖然一些學者如 Andy Kirkpatrick 和 Jennifer Jenkins（註）覺得英語是否說得和寫得地道並不重要，可是，我卻認為，我們能否意識到和分辨出一段英文話語是否自然、地道，還是很重要的。

回到篇首 blood donor centre 和 blood donation centre 的分別，雖然 blood donation centre 在字面意思上更為準確，但是我卻更喜歡 blood donor centre，因為它可以為捐血者（donor）帶來一點榮譽感呢！

最後一提的是，另一個在香港公共場合經常看見的詞——shroff。我們在公眾停車場經常看見這個詞，意思是「收銀處」。但初到香港的外地朋友都不明所以，詞典也找不到「收銀處」這解釋。除非我們認為 shroff 是地道的香港英語，否則還是用 cashier 較好。

註：Jenkins, Jennifer. (2007). *English as a Lingua Franca: Attitude and Identity*. Oxford: Oxford University Press.

Kirkpatrick, Andy. (2007). *World Englishes: Implications for International Communication and English Language Teaching*. New York: Cambridge University Press.

尋找地道的英語

「地道」的英文是 idiomatic，名詞是 idiomaticity，例如 His written English is accurate in terms of grammar but lacks idiomaticity。但 idiom 或 idiomatic expression 則解作「成語」或「習語」。

2 Add oil 是否英語？

不停衍化的英語

為 add oil 加油！

以下的語句中，你覺得哪些已經成為英語詞彙正式的一員？

Long time no see.	lai-see
Please dood your Octopus card.	chok
feng shui	jetso
kung fu	xiaolongbao
milk tea	t'ai chi
chow mein	qigong

你的判斷也許會分為三類：(1) 已經是標準英語詞彙；(2) 絕對不是英語詞彙；(3) 看情況而定。

外來語落戶英語的例子不少，例如以英語為母語的人士，偶然也會說 Long time no see，所以今天說 Long time no see 絕對不是問題。有些在英語文化中本來不存在的事物，今天也以音譯的形式，作為英語使用，例如日文的 sushi、teppanyaki、sukiyaki、tatami、kimono 等。從中文以音譯進入英語的例子也不少，較久遠的有 kowtow、feng shui、yin yang、t'ai chi 和 lai-see；近期的則有 guanxi（關係）、qigong（氣功）；較為地區化的有 xiaolongbao（小籠包）、cha chaan teng（茶餐廳）、chow mein（炒麵）；至於意譯的 milk tea（奶茶），在東南亞地方也可說是標準英語，但在英國的餐廳叫 milk tea，卻不要期望得到一杯我們熟悉的奶茶。當然，chow mein、cha chaan teng、milk tea 等例子目前仍可能集中於華人聚居的地方才會使用，而當地的英語人士也會聽得懂、看得懂；但如果有一天，這些事物進入外國人的日常生活，這些詞語也會成為標準英語；不要說像 sushi 和 feng shui 這些詞語了，就連我們熟悉的英語名詞 tea 和 pizza，其實也是源自外來語的呢！

那麼 add oil 處於哪個階段？我問身處香港的外籍朋友，add oil 是否英語時，他們有些斬釘截鐵地說不是，有些則不肯定，有些則表示，在和本地人溝通時，也會說 add oil 呢！如果有一天，add oil 正式成為英語的一員，我並不會感到意外，但暫時還只是港式英語。

近年香港人喜歡將一些粵語口語用英文字母拼寫出來，例如 chok、jetso、dood、chur 等。看得多，我們會否以為是英語呢？我到中學演講時，喜歡以 chok 和 jetso 為例，問學生這兩個詞是否英語既有的詞彙，有很多學生都說不清楚，但大約有三分之一的學生，卻很肯定的回答說，chok 和 jetso 原本就是英語！

近年學術界流行說 World Englishes，既然英語如此包容，那麼我們為何不創建 Hong Kong English，讓「港式英語」從此不再有貶義？這樣當我們說 I don't think so lor 的時候，也不會再覺得純為好玩，而是正正經經地在說英語。對此我並不是百分百贊同。記得某天收到銀行的宣傳信，邀請客戶為其八達通卡加入自動增值功能，其中提到 every time you dood your Octopus card ...，我的即時反應是：外國人會看得懂嗎？

尋找地道的英語

3 Question tag 有沒有標準答案？

活用 question tag 去表達想法

EQ 題

以下句子都附有附加疑問句 (question tag)，
哪些句子可以成立？

1　You know the answer, don't you?

2　You know the answer, do you?

3　You don't know the answer, do you?

4　You don't know the answer, don't you?

5　That's not Helen, is it?

6　That's not Helen, isn't she?

7　I'm wrong, amn't I?

8　I'm wrong, aren't I?

9　No one understands him, does he?

10　No one understands him, doesn't he?

11　No one understands him, do they?

12　No one understands him, don't they?

13　Everyone likes Michelle, doesn't he?

14　Everyone likes Michelle, don't they?

我們都希望文法規則像代數物理般齊齊整整，不要有例外情況，但是語言出現先於文法分析，而語言發展也非在實驗室中進行，故不能期望文法規律會十足工整。

　　以附加疑問句為例，最完美的情況當然是：

　　（一）凡主句的動詞是肯定的 (affirmative) 的，附加疑問句便是否定。例：You *know* the answer, *don't* you?

　　（二）凡主句的動詞是否定的，附加疑問句便是肯定。例：You *don't know* the answer, *do* you?

　　（三）主句的主語和附加疑問句的主語一模一樣。例：*You* know the answer, don't *you*?

　　如果出現這樣完美的情況，那麼只要把程式輸入電腦，電腦便可以替我們準確無誤的編寫出任何句子的附加疑問句了。

　　可是，有一些句子主句動詞是肯定式，但是主語卻有否定的意思，如 No one understands him；又有一些句子，主句的主語是單數形式，但意思卻是複數；更有一些因歷史原因，附加疑問句走出獨一無二的動詞；有時候，主句的主語在附加疑問句被相關詞代替，於是我們便有：

　　(1) No one understands him, do they?

　　(2) Everyone likes Michelle, don't they?

　　(3) I'm wrong, aren't I?

　　(4) That's not Helen, is it?

　　還有，下面 (5) 和 (6)，句 (5) 成立，但句 (6) 卻被唾棄，為甚麼？

　　(5) You know the answer, do you?

　　(6) You don't know the answer, don't you?

這正正是語言的美，數學非一即二，物理非黑即白，但人類語言卻容許多變，以表達複雜的思維和細緻的感情。數學是負負得正，但如果我說 I do not NOT love her，卻不等如 I love her。

You know the answer, don't you? 和 You don't know the answer, do you? 都是說話者有一個想法，然後請對方引證：

(7) You know the answer, don't you?（說話者覺得對方是知道答案的）

(8) You don't know the answer, do you?（說話者覺得對方是不知道答案的）

但是說話者也有不大肯定的時候，為了認真求證，他可能說句 (5) 的 You know the answer, do you?

那麼，邏輯上也可以有句 (6) 的出現：You don't know the answer, don't you?

但實際情況是，說話者用了一個不尋常的否定式主句（You don't know the answer），已反映了他已有頗肯定的想法，不需要求證。

語言還有更精彩的地方，就是在口語中加入各式語調（intonation）變化，從而衍生出更多細緻的含義，例如：

		期望的答案
	You know the answer, don't you?	Yes
語調	You know the answer, don't you?	
	降調 ↘　　　　　　　降調 ↘	

		期望的答案
	You don't know the answer, don't you?	No
語調	You don't know the answer, don't you?	
	降調 ↘　　　　　　　降調 ↘	

語調	You know the answer, don't you? You know the answer, don't you? 降調 ↘　　　　　升調 ↗	期望的答案 Yes or No
語調	You don't know the answer, do you? You don't know the answer, do you? 降調 ↘　　　　　升調 ↗	期望的答案 Yes or No
語調	You know the answer, do you? You know the answer, do you? 降調 ↘　　　　　升調 ↗	期望的答案 Yes

　　總而言之，學習附加疑問句如果只埋首其表面形式，而不去發掘其變化及傳意功能，便不能充分發揮語言的力量。

知多一點點

下面的例子屬特殊的附加疑問句：

1　He may know the answer, mightn't he?

2　He used to work here, didn't/did he?

3　Let's go home, shall we?

4 考起老師的 my favourite animal

教學上的句子與地道的説法

EQ 題

請從以下句子中，圈選你認為正確的句子。

1 My favourite animal is dog.

2 My favourite animal is dogs.

3 My favourite animal is a dog.

4 My favourite animal is the dog.

5 My favourite animals are dogs.

6 My favourite food is hot dog.

7 My favourite food is hot dogs.

8 My favourite food is a hot dog.

9 My favourite food is the hot dog.

10 Dog are my favourite animal.

11 Dogs are my favourite animal.

12 Hot dog is my favourite food.

13 The hot dog is my favourite food.

14 Hot dogs are my favourite food.

常有英語教師問，到底 favourite 後面該接上單數還是複數名詞呢？為甚麼會有這個問題？一般情況下，他們先在教科書看到包含 favourite 一詞的句子，例如：

(1) My favourite story is Cinderella.

教師解釋句子意思後，就囑學生以 favourite 一詞造句，但當學生寫了以下的句子時，部分教師卻感到困惑，不知如何處理：

(2) My favourite animal is dogs.

(3) My favourite animal is dog.

根據英文文法，句子中的主語與動詞形式必須一致 (subject-verb agreement)，故此句子的前半部分 My favourite animal is 並沒有問題。可是，is 後面是否可接上複數名詞，例如 dogs 呢？如要用單數名詞，又是否要根據英文文法，加上冠詞 a，讓句子變成 My favourite animal is a dog？

上述例子顯示英文文法只是通則 (generalization)，遇上特殊情況可能會幫不上忙。以英語為母語的人士，對上述問題也有不同的看法，有人認為 dogs 既然是泛指狗隻這類動物，而不是指特定的一群狗隻，那麼就以 dogs 來表示單數的概念吧！另一些人則認為，與其糾纏於主語與動詞形式必須一致這項規條，不如簡單的將句子改為 Dogs are my favourite animal，這樣便輕鬆解決了問題。不錯，這確實可以避免了文法上的尷尬，但卻失去了以 My favourite animal 作為句子主語的特定傳意功能。

還有另一個建議，就是説 My favourite animal is the dog。英文冠詞 the 有時可用於泛指某類事物，例如：

(4) The panda is in danger of extinction.

(5) The tiger is a fierce animal.

句子中的 the panda，不是指某隻熊貓，而是指所有的熊貓；同理，the tiger 也是泛指所有老虎。故此説 My favourite animal is the dog 也是一個不錯的選擇。

　　討論至此，還有一個問題：不錯，以 My favourite 起首的句子，理論上可以存在，但在日常生活中又有多常見呢？我在英國國家語料庫（British National Corpus）鍵入 my favourite，找到以下例子：

(6)　My favourite subject is (English).

(7)　My favourite character is …

(8)　My favourite country is …

(9)　My favourite player is …

(10)　My favourite person is …

　　在上述選例中，favourite 後面接的名詞，都是單一的人和事，而非像 animal、food 一樣，泛指一類事物。由此我們可以推斷，文法教學和練習中的某些説法，只是理論上存在，在現實生活中並不常見。如果要説自己最喜歡吃熱狗，較常用的説法可能是 I love eating hot dogs the most；同理，要説自己最喜歡狗，何不説 I love dogs the most，而 要 糾 纏 於 My favourite animal is（dog/dogs/a dog/the dog）呢？

問題評析

　　文法上，篇首問題的句子 3、4、5、8、9、11、13、14 都是對的。句子 3、5、8 的意思不清晰，在一些很特殊的情況下也許説得通；句子 9 和 13 的對錯取決於我們可否接受用 the 去泛指熱狗。至於句子 2 和 7，看上去有點奇怪，但很多以英語為母語的人接受這種用法。

5 告示獨有的語言

要簡潔還是要「正確」？

這則告示的英文版是給狗兒看的嗎？

在西貢海濱公園看到前頁圖中的告示牌時，第一個反應是覺得它很搞笑。首先，圖示連狗兒的排泄物也畫了出來，實在引人發噱，真的需要如此清晰嗎？其次，告示的英文版 Do not foul on public area，似乎是寫給狗兒看的呢！

中文告示請狗主不要讓狗隻隨處便溺，這沒有問題。英文告示用了祈使句型 (imperative)，這句型隱含了主語 You：

(1) Stop talking. → You stop talking.

(2) Drive carefully. → You drive carefully.

(3) Don't run. → You don't run.

(4) Don't foul in public areas. → You don't foul in public areas.

看看例 (4)，便明白告示的意思，是請大家不要在公共地方便溺啊！除非告示是給狗隻看的。

用英文表達「勿讓狗隻隨處便溺」的意思，一般會說 No fouling；更清楚的話，可以說 No dog fouling。

也許你會說，No fouling 豈非也是衝着人類（即狗主）而說？但 Don't foul 和 No fouling 有着微妙的分別。Don't foul 是祈使句，隱含了主語 You，但 No fouling 不是祈使句，它只是指出不要出現的事情，No (dog) fouling 就是不要有狗隻隨處便溺的情況發生。

誠然，No cycling、No kite flying 等告示，實際都是針對人類發出的，但句式上沒有這個必然性。No fouling 和 No dog fouling 都是英語世界裏的慣用說法，把告示置於遛狗的地方，牠們的主人見到都會明白其意思，不會誤會是叫他們自己不要隨處便溺！

我在山頂看過另一則告示，對狗主的指示就十分清楚：

應帶備足夠報紙或膠袋，將狗隻糞便包好並放入狗糞收集箱或垃圾箱
Take enough newapapers or plastic bags with you when you walk your dog. Wrap up the dog's faeces with newspapers or plastic bags and place it into the Dog Excreta Collection Bin or rubbish bin.

　　然而，這則告示的毛病卻正是過分清晰，中文版本是否需要這樣清晰，讓讀者自行判斷好了，但以英語為母語的人士看到英文版時，想必莞爾。因為在英語世界中，要表達類似的意思，只須用六個字，那就是：Please clean up after your dog。

　　英文告示有其慣用寫法，不要由中文直譯過去。下面的告示，為甚麼一些指示以 Please 開始，其他的卻沒有？

嚴禁吸煙
No Smoking

請勿攜犬入內
Please - No Dogs

嚴禁擺賣
No Hawking

請勿踏單車
Please - No Cycling

後來看看中文版，才明白作者的想法：

(6) 嚴禁 …… → No …

(7) 請勿 …… → Please — No …

英文有這樣的分別嗎？當然沒有。英文告示有其習用的語言，切忌直譯。

6 「利是」的浮想

母語人士的英文一定正確？

究竟是 red packet 還是 red pocket？

上面兩個告示出現在同一商場，第一次出現時，「利是」的英譯是 red pocket，一年之後卻換成了 red packet，到底哪個才對？

我問過本地一些母語非英語的人士，他們大多認為用 red packet 才對。可是當我問以英語為母語的人士（以下稱為「外籍人士」）時，他們大都選擇 red pocket，並認為 red packet 有誤。有些人還煞有介事的解釋，說利是看上去像襯衣的口袋，所以應為 red pocket。究竟外籍人士的解釋是否正確呢？

有這樣的疑問，是因為想起之前發生的一件事。大家可能有聽過以下說法：

(1) You are what you eat.

(2) You are what you read.

這兩句話的意思，是你吃甚麼，或閱讀甚麼，就會漸漸變成一個怎樣的人。有一年，我模仿這個說法，把給予師訓學員的功課定名為 You teach who you are，請他們反思自己的教學，以及自己的個性和價值觀念之間的關係。其中一名學員把功課給予外籍同事過目，這位外籍同事看不出標題背後的含義，將它改為 You teach the way you are，這當然也對，但卻失去了原來的神韻。其實美國教育家 Parker J. Palmer 在他的著作（註）中，經常使用 We teach who we are，去表達教師自我反思的重要性。

事實上，英語知識浩如煙海，就算是外籍人士也不會懂得全部。例如教育界有 teach to the test 這一說法，意指教學時只就着考試範圍而教。有一次我投稿至一份學術期刊，文稿中用到此一說法，審稿員竟以為我犯了文法錯誤，要求我更正！

有一段時間，我迷上了英語警匪劇集。在劇集中，當警探抵達兇案現場時，通常會向比他早到達的警探問：

What do you got? (這宗案件是甚麼？用香港粵語的説法，是「乜嘢料」。)

起初我以為自己聽錯，但看了很多集，發現劇中人全都是這樣説的，於是我問一位外籍人士這種説法有多普遍，怎知他認為我是把 What have you got? 誤當成 What do you got?。終於有一次，我見到字幕打出來的果真就是 What do you got?。

英語發展至今，出現了各類型的演變，例如區域 (regional) 上的、語域 (register) 上的。英語為母語的人士，其語言覺識 (language awareness) 未必一定高，英國學者 Rod Bolitho、Brian Tomlinson、Scott Thornbury 和香港學者 Stephen Andrews 對此都有相同看法。他們其中一個工作重點，就是幫助當英語教師的外籍人士，提高對英語的覺識哩！

註：Parker, J. Palmer (1983). *To know as we are known: Education as a spiritual journey*. New York: HarperCollins.

某網站列出 12 個外籍人士最常犯的錯誤，以下是其中三條，大家知道正確的答案嗎？

1　Which of the following words is possessive?

　　A　their　　　　　B　there　　　　　C　they're

2　What is the past tense of the verb 'lie'?

　　A　lay　　　　　B　laid

3　Which of these words would you use to complete the sentence '___ cold outside'?

　　A　It's　　　　　B　Its

7 不要隨便叫人 touch and go

學懂地道的説法

各種語文均有其特定的表達形式，如果說英語時，先在腦中構想中文句子，然後將句子逐字翻譯成英文，很容易會弄出笑話。公眾地方的廣播或告示，更應特別注意。先前港鐵廣播請乘客出入閘口時插卡，英文版本為：

Passengers with single-journey smart tickets should use the blue gate. Touch and go; insert and exit.

為了簡潔，拍票入閘給說成是 touch and go。不幸英文 touch 有不正當觸摸別人的引伸義，與 go 合用，彷彿是請別人做不正當的行為！其實要說拍票入閘，用地道的說法 tap in 便可以了。新加坡地鐵的用語，就是 tap in（即拍卡入閘）和 tap out（即拍卡出閘）。英文類似的簡潔說法，就是 clock in 和 clock out，指上班時打卡開工，下班時打卡離開。

下圖的告示以 warming notice 為標題，這應該是從中文「溫馨提示」譯過來的吧。Warming 固然是錯誤的文法，但也沒有必要修正為 Warm。我還見過 friendly reminder 和 gentle reminder，其實地道的英語不過簡簡單單的說 Reminder 或 Notice，前面並不需要加上任何形容詞。

逐字翻譯，一不小心便會鬧出笑話，大家發現以下告示的問題嗎？

中文告示通常叮囑別人小心這樣、小心那樣，英文有時候是 Beware of …，有時候是 Mind …，但兩者不能互換。圖中兩種說法在同一餐廳出現，哪種說法才妥當？

原來請別人注意梯級或地面濕滑，以防不小心滑倒，英文的說法是：

Mind the steps.

Mind the slippery floor.

後者也可以說 Caution: Slippery floor 或 Caution: Floor may be slippery。

　　逐字翻譯，還有可能會引起紛爭。中文說「停車等候會被檢控」，雖然沒有標明主語，但憑語境，不難猜到誰會被檢控，可是英文卻不能這樣模糊。以下告示關於非法停車等候，我常常想，被控的車主或司機，會否以英文指示不妥當，作為在法庭抗辯的理由呢？

　　總括來說，說好外語，切忌依靠逐字翻譯。

8 百變的名詞和動詞

詞性要變就變

Seat 可否作動詞使用？

圖中的告示有一個問題，那就是 don't 之後的 seat 應改為 sit，即 Please don't sit（on the steps）或 No sitting。

　　可能有人會想，seat 之所以不能用於 don't 之後，是因為 seat 是名詞，但其實 seat 也可作動詞用。To seat someone 是指將某人安排坐在某個位置，一些高級餐廳門口會貼出 Please wait to be seated 的告示，意思是請顧客等候安排入座。

　　我讀小學時，老師在英文課堂上花了相當的時間教授詞類，說每個英文單詞都有其傳統的詞類，我們一眾學生花了不少時間記誦單詞的詞類。

　　但近年大眾對詞類的規限開始沒那麼執著，也許很多人不知道 Please email me 中的動詞 email，其實經過以下的進化階段：

Electronic mail → E-mail（名詞）→ e-mail（名詞）→ email（名詞）→ email（名詞及動詞）

　　那天有舊生問我，說 Please whatsapp me 是否正確。如果比較 email 和 whatsapp 的詞義，不難猜到答案。事實上，和通訊有關的科技名詞，例如 email、whatsapp、telephone、fax、text、skype 等，都因大眾頻密使用，很快就成為了動詞。今時今日，以下的說法絕對可以接受：

(1) To telephone/fax/email/text/skype/whatsapp someone

　　其實，兩大社交網絡 Facebook 和 Twitter，均可作動詞使用，例如 Please facebook me。但要留意 Twitter 的動詞是 tweet 而不是 twit，例如 I am tweeting。

有些英文單詞，傳統上已有名詞和動詞的形式，而且兩者拼法相同，例如 litter 和 trash，這些英文單詞通常以名詞的形式使用，但偶然作為動詞使用，會有不同的效果，試看看以下兩句：

(2) My boss likes to trash my ideas. I really hate him.

(3) That online forum is littered with negative and rude comments.

英文單詞由名詞演變成動詞並非唯一的方向，現在愈來愈多動詞也可當作名詞使用，常見的例子有：

(4) a hot **buy**（熱賣產品）

(5) a good **read**（好讀物）

(6) a brilliant **save**（精彩的救球）

(7) a historical **feel**（歷史的感覺）

以下的常用語，也是把動詞當作名詞使用的例子：

(8) Have a **listen** (to this song).

(9) Give it a **try**.

(10) Have a **go**.

(11) Give it a **think**.

(12) Have a **read** (of the newspaper).

(13) Good **eats**（美味的食物）

詞類演化是一個約定俗成的過程，例如 ask 是否可作名詞使用，解作「期望」、「要求」呢？傳統英文有 a big ask，指一件很難實現的事情，但 ask 不能單獨作名詞使用。不過最近已有人將 ask 當作 request、expectation 使用，例如：

(14) My ask is for 20 days off per year.（我要求每年有二十天假期。）

不過也有人反對將 ask 作名詞使用，Facebook 上甚至有稱為 Stop Using 'Ask' as a Noun 的群組呢！

　　語言不斷發展，語文運用要夠「潮」，便要加強自己的語言觸覺。

9 Usually 是否比 often 更頻密？
頻率副詞沒有固定頻率

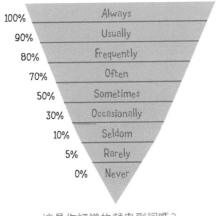

這是你認識的頻率副詞嗎？

英文有一組詞語，包括 always、sometimes、often 和 seldom 等，都有副詞的特性，就是用來修飾句子中動詞片語所描述的事情，意思都和事情有多頻密發生有關。在句式上，這些詞通常放在主語之後，例如 He always/ sometimes/often brings her flowers。

　　因此，文法書都把這些詞歸納為副詞一類，稱為頻率副詞 (adverbs of frequency)。但是在教學上，這些副詞可否像前頁圖中顯示，以頻密程度為基礎排列成像下面的一個體系？

always → usually → frequently → often → sometimes → occasionally → seldom → rarely → never

　　我翻查了數本文法參考書，發覺它們沒有以這樣的方式處理這個問題；但有趣的是，在很多英文教學材料中，都有這樣的解釋。我在網上，便找到很多像文首的解釋圖，文法練習書甚至會有下面的練習：

	M	T	W	T	F	S	S
John plays the piano …		✓		✓		✓	✓
Sam plays football …		✓	✓	✓	✓	✓	
Winnie plays badminton …	✓	✓	✓	✓	✓	✓	✓

John _____ plays the piano.　　（答案：often）

Sam _____ plays football.　　（答案：usually）

Winnie _____ plays badminton.　　（答案：always）

　　頻率副詞真的可以和量化了的頻率配對使用嗎？例如真的有90%用 usually，50%用 sometimes 這規定嗎？

在文法描述上，我們傾向將相關的概念歸納在一起；在教學上，我們傾向把文法歸納成簡單的規則，以方便解釋和學習，經過調整後的一套文法規則稱為教學語法 (pedagogical grammar)。教學語法有其實際需要，但有時也會因過分簡化 (oversimplification) 而扭曲了相關的文法概念。就以頻率副詞為例，雖然它們的確和頻密程度有關，但請看看下面 How often … 的對話：

> Teacher (to 5 students): 'How often do you go to the library?'
>
> Student A: 'I *always* go to the library.'
>
> Student B: 'I *usually* go to the library.'
>
> Student C: 'I *often* go to the library.'
>
> Student D: 'I *sometimes* go to the library.'
>
> Student E: 'I go to the library *once a week*.'

你認為哪一個學生是答其所問？

不錯，只有 Student E 在純粹講頻率，Student A 至 D 的答案都有點答非所問，但這正好提醒我們，頻率副詞不單是在表示頻率，而有其他的意思和傳意功能。我們再看看下面的對話：

> Interviewer: 'Which supermarket do you go to?'
>
> Mrs A: 'I usually go to Supermarket X, but sometimes I go to Supermarket Y.'
>
> Interviewer: 'What about you, Mrs B?'
>
> Mrs B: 'I always go to Supermarket Y. Their staff are more friendly.'
>
> Interviewer: 'How often do you go to Supermarket Y, Mrs B?'
>
> Mrs B: 'Once a fortnight.'

這對話反映出頻率副詞所表示的「頻率」，只是相對的概念。而且，頻率副詞往往有其他的傳意目的，例如 Mrs A 說 I usually go to Supermarket X 時，她不是純粹說往 Supermarket 的頻率，而是暗示她有時會有不同的行動；Mrs B 實際上只是兩星期才上超級市場一次，但她說 I always go to Supermarket Y，用意是強調 Supermarket Y 是她的唯一選擇。

頻率副詞只可以粗略地顯示頻率，並不表示量化了的頻率，而且採用時要考慮語境，要充分掌握頻率副詞，靠的仍然是對文法的敏感度。

知多一點點

以下的真實句子來自 British National Corpus（英國國家語料庫），句中的 usually 其實和頻率沒有太大關係：

1 House agents are not usually poets.
2 The exit is by the ladies and usually blocked with beer crates.
3 I'm not certain about the buses, I usually cycle …

4 The Consul's house was where the meetings were usually held.

10 句子非完整不可？

不要成為句式的奴隸

EQ 題

以下的閱讀理解題，四個答案在意思上全屬正確，你認為哪一個答案可給予滿分？

Why does John go to the library every day?

A He likes reading.

B Because he likes reading.

C It is because he likes reading.

D John goes to the library every day because he likes reading.

之前有英文報紙曾刊登某讀者的來函，寫信人指考評局英文科考試的答題簿上寫的 Please do not take away 屬文法錯誤。讀者認為，take 是及物動詞（transitive verb），後面必須加上賓語 (object)，例如 this answer book，才算是一個完整句子。

老師教授英語寫作時，總會千叮萬囑，着同學寫完整句子（complete sentence）。在學校作文訓練時，這提示一般適用，但語言運用還要顧及場合，是否完整句子並非唯一考慮。

以 Please do not take away 為例，句子出現在答題簿上，不要拿走的是答題簿，意義十分明顯，加上賓語，變成 Please do not take this answer book away，反而顯得累贅。這情況等於在洗手間的提示 Please flush after use，不須用完整句子的說法 Please flush the toilet after use。

另一例子是學校閱讀理解練習中問「為甚麼」的題目。問題以 Why 起首，回答時當然就會說出理由。Because … 已經足以把要說的原因都說了，不必硬性規定學生回答說 It is because …，或覆述問題一遍，以期答案是完整句子。其實很多時候，連 Because 也可以省略，因為對話雙方都清楚答案是為問題給予理由，沒必要以 Because 一詞作引子。

我讀小學時，部分老師不單要求學生在答案中寫上 It is because 或 Because，更要把問題中的文字抄在答案中，認為那才是最完整的答案。例如：

(1) Why does John go to the library every day?

(2) John goes to the library every day because he likes reading.

今天已少有人要求學生作這類長答。有一次我和一班在職教師學員討論這個話題，其中一位說，他和英文科主任討論，科主任聲稱所有公開試評分參考都指明答案必須為完整句子。聽到學員的轉述讓我嚇了一跳，我立刻找來所有公開試評分參考查看，卻沒有看到這項規定。

從上面兩個例子，不難發現語境會影響到人們寫和說的時候是否採用完整句子。我在美國的地鐵車廂內，見到扶手旁寫有 Please hold on。雖然 hold on 可解作「等一下」或「堅持」，但出現在扶手旁，hold on 的意思已很明顯，不須像香港交通工具上說的 Hold the handrail and stand still 那麼累贅。

在公函中常見以下句子：

(3) I would be grateful if you could fill in the form and return to us on or before …

有朋友問句子中 return 後面的賓語 it 可否省略。這不易決定。return 甚麼，意思很明顯，也可解釋為 fill in and return the form to us 的另一說法，但如果要「安全」，不被挑戰，還是保留 it 字為妙。

知多一點點

已故語言哲學家 Paul Grice 提出著名的合作原則（Cooperative Principle），以解釋人們溝通的行為，其中一個守則是切題 (be relevant)。故此如果甲問乙 Why，乙無論作何種回答，一般情況下都可理解為正在提出理由。

走進詞語的密林

11 「可以用」還是「可以被人用」?

是否被動還要看詞義

Your device is ready to use?
Your device is ready to be used?

電腦視窗安裝新軟件後，螢幕的右下角會出現提示 Your device is ready to use。有臉書朋友問，這個句子是否應改為 Your device is ready to be used？

為甚麼朋友會有此一問？他的想法顯然是使用軟件的是我們，而不是軟件去使用某些東西，故此應該改用 to be used 這個被動結構。

這種想法不無道理。英文的確經常透過文法去表達主事者和受事者的關係，常見的方法是利用詞序，例如：

(1) The man killed the lion.

(2) The lion killed the man.

誰殺了誰，完全由詞序表達。如果是獅子被殺了，但我們想將獅子保留作為句子的主語，那麼動詞便要改用被動式 was killed，以表達獅子才是受事者。不過這並非必然，且看以下兩個句子：

(3) John asked Peter to see a doctor.

(4) John promised Peter to see a doctor.（註）

這兩個句子的結構相同，但在每個句子中，是誰要去看醫生呢？不錯，句子 (3) 是 Peter 要去看醫生，句子 (4) 則是 John 要去看。為甚麼會這樣？

留意 (3) 和 (4) 兩句的唯一分別在於所用的動詞，可以推斷，這兩個句子是由字詞的語義 (semantics) 界定了人物的關係，而非由句式決定。可再多看以下例子：

(5) Tom is easy to please.

(6) Tom is eager to please.

Tom 究竟是主事者還是受事者，完全由 easy 和 eager 兩個形容詞決定。在句子 (5) 中，Tom 是被人討好的對象，而在句子 (6) 中，急於取悅他人的是 Tom。

如果我們將句子 (6) 的形容詞再改為 ready，即：

(7) Tom is ready to please.

那麼 Tom 是主事者還是受事者？答案是 Tom 是主事（to please，討好）的人。但將 ready 轉為 difficult（即 Tom is difficult to please），主語 Tom 又變成了受事者！

因此，我們發現，原先認為文法中的句子詞序 (word order) 決定句子的意思，這個概念是需要修正的。在某些句式中，是相關字詞的詞義決定句子的意思。

在一些特別的情況下，句子的意思會模糊了，語言學 (linguistics) 的經典例句是：

(8) The chicken is ready to eat.

究竟是說，雞去吃東西，還是雞被吃呢？兩個意思都同時存在。

現在再比較以下三句，看看哪一句是解不通的：

(9) Tom is difficult to please.

(10) The problem is difficult to solve.

(11) Peter is difficult to solve the problem.

不錯，(11) 是常見的錯誤，我們也許猜到其意思，但這句英文卻語意不清。

回到 Your device is ready to use，改為 Your device is ready to be used 固然可以，但從詞義角度考量，Your device is ready to use 也絕無問題。

註：To promise someone to do something 的結構現已獲廣泛應用，但不少人仍然較喜歡傳統的用法：John promised Peter that he would see a doctor。

12 Commence 是開始還是被開始？

善用主動格動詞

啟市？被啟市？

在這個告示中，will be closed 沒有問題，可是 will be commenced 讀起來卻有點怪怪的，為甚麼？

要想知道原因，請大家先比較下面兩組句子，看看當中的動詞有甚麼特性：

A	B
(1) Sam *is playing*.	Sue *is playing* computer games.
(2) Fred *was eating*.	Fiona *was eating* a hot dog.
(3) Mum *is cooking*.	Dad *is cooking* a delicious meal for the kids.
(4) These students *read* every day.	Those students *read* the newspaper every day.

兩組句子共採用了四個動詞，分別是 play、eat、cook 和 read。在 A 組中，動詞不接賓語（留意最後一句的 every day 是狀語 (adverbial) 而非賓語）。在 B 組中，動詞後則接賓語。為甚麼這四個動詞同時適用於這兩種句型呢？這和動詞的及物性 (transitivity) 有關。play、eat、cook 和 read 這四個動詞，既可作及物動詞，同時也可作不及物動詞使用。

留意並非所有動詞均能同時擁有及物和不及物兩種屬性，英文中有很多動詞，只能作及物 (transitive) 動詞或不及物動 (transitive) 詞使用。這解釋了為甚麼 C 組的句子妥當，D 組的句子則有問題：

C (✓)	D (✗)
(5) He *is listening*.	He *is needing*.
(6) The children *slept*.	The children *had*.
(7) Scientists *think*.	The scientist *discovered*.
(8) I *pray*.	I *like*.

及物動詞一般可用於被動句，play 和 eat 既然可作及物動詞使用，故此也適用於被動語態，例如：

(9) These computer games *are played* by many people in this country.

(10) Hot dogs *are* seldom *eaten* in that country.

那麼，文初告示中的 close 和 commence，又是否及物動詞呢？不錯，close 和 commence 確是及物動詞，故此適用於被動語態，例如：

(11) We *will close* the shop on 31 December.（主動）

(12) The shop *will be closed* on 31 December.（被動）

(13) We *will commence* business on 7 January.（主動）

(14) Business *will be commenced* on 7 January.（被動）

可是 will be commenced 聽起來並不自然，為甚麼？原來 commence 屬文法分類中的主動格動詞 (ergative verb)（又稱「作格動詞」），這類動詞同時擁有及物和不及物的屬性，故此也適用於被動語態。除 commence 外，其他的例子有 resume、begin、finish、continue 等，例如：

(15) The programme *will continue* at 7 o'clock.（主動）

(16) The programme *will be continued* at 7 o'clock.（被動）

(17) Service *will resume* next Monday.（主動）

(18) Service *will be resumed* next Monday.（被動）

但是除非有特殊原因，主動格動詞一般應用於主動語態，因此 Service will resume next Monday 比 Service will be resumed next Monday 自然；同樣，表示「啟市」，說 Business will commence … 便可以了。

使用主動格動詞時，不要無故採用被動式，因主動式會令意思較生動。猜猜美國最大網上書店 Amazon 通知顧客訂單何時付運，會用以下兩句中的哪一句？

(19) Your order will ship in 7 days.

(20) Your order will be shipped in 7 days.

不錯，他們使用的，正是句 (19) Your order will ship in 7 days。

13 為何要小心 Beware of？

Mind 和 Beware of 的微妙分別

要小心的是甚麼？

在香港，中文告示一般是提醒別人小心這樣、小心那樣。或許是出於這個原因，人們將告示譯作英文時，也一律以 beware of 起首，而沒察覺到 beware of 在英文中有特別的用法。有一次，我在海洋公園就見到兩位外籍遊客看見 Beware of the steps 這個告示後竊竊私語。

以下有八個句子，均以 beware of 起首。請各位判斷哪些句子合乎正確的用法：

(1) Beware of pickpockets.

(2) Beware of falling objects.

(3) Beware of drunk drivers.

(4) Beware of the dog.

(5) Beware of the slippery floor.

(6) Beware of the steps.

(7) Hot food. Beware of your fingers.

(8) Beware of your head.

各位想到了嗎？不錯，第 (1)、(2)、(3)、(4) 句都是正確的。這些句子跟其餘四句有甚麼不同呢？

Pickpockets、falling objects、drunk drivers 和 the dog，都是有可能出現並且會為我們帶來危險的事物（例如 pickpockets、falling objects、drunk drivers），或已經出現而有可能會傷害我們的事物（例如那隻兇惡的狗）。但是，the slippery floor 和 the steps 等，都是客觀上存在，但不會主動傷害我們的事物；如果我們受了損傷，那是因為我們自己不小心，而非受到這些事物的攻擊，故此不應說 Beware of ...。另一例子是有關港鐵車廂與月台之間的空隙，港鐵的提示是說 Mind the gap (between the train and the platform)，而不是 Beware of the gap。

大家現在應該明白，為甚麼 Beware of your head 和 Beware of your fingers 會引人發噱，因為有可能帶來危險的，並不是我們自己的頭和手指啊！所以要提醒別人小心自己周圍的事物，應該說 Mind …，例如 Mind your head、Mind your fingers、Mind the steps 等。另一說法是 Caution: …（要留意的客觀事物），例如：

(9)　Caution: Hot food

(10)　Caution: Slippery floor

(11)　Caution: Floor may be slippery

　　所以大家可以想像，為甚麼某天早上，我在海濱花園看見下面的告示時，竟然如此欣慰，因為它沒有說 *Beware of fishing equipment 啊！

　　其實詞典一般只會提供單詞的解釋，或一、兩個例句，例如詞典中 beware of 的解釋是 used to warn someone of danger or difficulty，單憑這個解釋，便有可能說出上面第 (5) 至 (8) 有誤的句子。要更深入了解一個用語的意思和用法，可上網查閱語料庫 (corpus)，例如下面 beware of 的句子，便是從 British National Corpus（英國國家語料庫）

中找到的，這些都是從日常生活中選輯出來的句子，有助加深我們對 beware of 的認識：

(12) Beware of those who want to take over the organizer's job.

(13) Beware of flogging an issue too hard.

(14) Beware of moving the whole body towards the sail.

(15) Beware of poison oak.

(16) Beware of the bull.

(17) Beware of prolonged high altitude camping.

(18) Beware of windows.

上面最後一句，說話者顯然對窗戶存有戒心，覺得它們會帶來危險，故此說 Beware of windows；但如果已經有一扇破了的窗戶在那裏，要提醒別人留意，還是應該說 Mind the window。

知多一點點 ─────────────────────────────

現時主要的語料庫有 British National Corpus、American National Corpus、Oxford English Corpus 和 International Corpus of English，其中一些需要先行下載，或購買有關光碟，British National Corpus 可在網上直接使用。當然簡單的 Google search，有時也有一些參考價值。

14 錢為何不可以數？

不可數名詞的真正意義

英文的名詞有所謂 countable nouns 和 uncountable nouns 之分，學校老師和一些文法書，會順理成章的將 countable nouns 和 uncountable nouns 解作可數和不可數的名詞，教 uncountable nouns 時，一般會以 air 和 water 等詞為例子，解釋不可數的概念。

記得小學時聽到老師這樣的解釋，總覺牽強，為甚麼 bread 不可數？我們不是可以數一個麵包、兩個麵包嗎？Money 為甚麼不可數？我們不是可以數一元、兩元、三元嗎？

其實 bread 代表一類食物，這個名詞本身並不等同於我們說的菠蘿包、雞尾包、牛角包等，要說這些一個一個的麵包，英文另有 bun、roll、muffin、scone、croissant、sandwich 等字，這些都是所謂的 countable nouns。所以嚴格來說，不是麵包不可以一個一個的數，而是 bread 這個名詞，泛指這類用麵粉烘烤而成的食品，不是指一個一個的麵包，因而是不可數的。同理，一張一張的紙幣 (banknote) 和一個一個的錢幣 (coin) 當然可以數，但 money 一詞是泛指金錢，不是指可數的紙幣和硬幣 (註)。

從上述例子我們可以看到，一個名詞是 countable 還是 uncountable，不是一個形式文法 (formal grammar) 的問題，而是有關它本身真正的詞義。Furniture 之所以是 uncountable，因為它泛指該類型物件，名詞本身不等同於枱、櫈、牀等這些絕對可以逐一數數的物件。

正因如此，英語中有大量既是 countable 又是 uncountable 的名詞。當 change 代表宇宙間一個現象，例如 Change is inevitable（變幻是無可避免的），change

就是 uncountable noun；但如果 change 指的是具體的改變，那麼它就是 countable noun，例如我們會說 I have made a few changes to your design（我對你的設計作了數個改動）。其他既是 uncountable noun 又是 countable noun 的例子還有 thought、connection、fruit 和 life。以 life 為例，泛指生命時是 uncountable noun，說到十條人命時則變成 countable，寫作 ten lives；chicken 指雞肉時是 uncountable，指一隻一隻的雞時則變成 countable。

傳統英文文法將名詞分為 countable nouns 和 uncountable nouns，想來只是取其方便的說法，由於 countable 和 uncountable 兩字的確可能會引起概念上的誤解，近年一些文法書改以 count nouns 一詞代替 countable nouns，用 mass nouns 代替 uncountable nouns。

事實上，我們與其死記硬背一個名詞是否可數或不可數，不如深入了解這名詞的真正意義。譬如我們知道 homework 是泛指家課，便不會說 *three homeworks，而會說 three assignments、three homework assignments 或 three pieces of homework；知道 advice 是泛指忠告，便懂得說 He gave me a lot of suggestions，而非 *He gave me a lot of advices。

註：在法律文件中，money 可以複數形式 moneys/monies 出現；water 用於複數時 (waters) 指海域。

15 應該說 travel happy 還是 travel happily？

游走形容詞與副詞之間

圖中的廣告，travel happy 是否應該改作
travel happily？

根據英語文法的分類，travel 是實義動詞 (lexical verb)，和 is、am、are 等助動詞有別。我們通常用副詞 (adverb) 來修飾或補充實義動詞，例如：

(1) He runs *quickly*.

(2) She is walking *slowly*.

(3) They lived happily.

若是這樣，廣告中的形容詞 happy 似乎應改作 happily。

當然，英文有一些連繫動詞 (copular verb) 的確是與形容詞一起使用，例如：

(4) He *looks* happy.

(5) I *feel* cold.

(6) It *seemed* unreal.

(7) The sentence sounds OK.

這些句子中，動詞的補語 (complement) 的確是形容詞而不是副詞，故此我們不能説 *The man became angrily、*I feel safely 或 *She got richly。

但 travel 又不是連繫動詞，我們又怎能接受 travel happy 的説法？

首先，請比較下表中 A、B 兩組句子，嘗試看出兩者之間的分別：

A	B
(8) He spelt my name *wrongly*.	He spelt my name *wrong*.
(9) Send your application to the manager *directly*.	Send your application to the manager *direct*.
(10) They said it *rightly*.	You guessed *right*.
(11) Please tie the parcel *tightly*.	Please hold *tight*.
(12) She likes to travel *lightly*.	She likes to travel *light*.

B 組句子中的斜體字，雖然看起來像形容詞，但其實都是副詞。兩組句子雖然意義大致相同，但重點卻有微妙的分別。He spelt my name wrongly 說的是他如何拼寫出我的名字，He spelt my name wrong 則強調拼寫的結果，說他把我的名字拼錯了。Tie the parcel tightly 是說如何綁好包裹，Please hold tight 中的 tight 則較強調狀態。總括來說，以 -ly 結尾的副詞一般用於描述事情如何進行，所以這一類的副詞又稱為方式副詞 (adverb of manner)。B 組句子中的副詞，說的則是某種特質、狀態或結果。

　　然而，happy 又 不 像 wrong、direct、right、tight、light 等同時是副詞，travel 和 happy 兩字真的可以走在一起嗎？語文運用，有時候會跳過文法的規限，造出特別的效果。下表中，D 組的句子在動詞後用形容詞而不用副詞，試看看這種用法的效果：

C	D
(13) Act *smartly* during the interview.	Act *smart* during the interview.
(14) To maintain good health, eat *healthily*.	To maintain good health, eat *healthy*.
(15) Book your holiday with us and travel *happily*.	Book your holiday with us and travel *happy*.

　　看過 (13) 和 (14) 之後，大家也許覺得 (15) 的 travel happy，不但可以接受，而且有其巧妙的意思。

　　作家林沛理曾談及已故蘋果創辦人喬布斯的經驗 (註)。蘋果的廣告團隊原本的建議，是符合文法規則的

註：林沛理 (2013)。《私想》。台北：二魚文化事業有限公司。

Think differently，但喬布斯力排眾議，堅持要用 Think different，結果這成為蘋果膾炙人口的宣傳口號。林沛理指出喬布斯取 Think different 而捨 Think differently，是以身作則，教人「另闢蹊徑，跳出框框想問題」。

至於我們常人，有沒有打破文法的勇氣，別人又懂不懂欣賞，則是另一回事了。

16 小心多重意義的 self-

了解詞義還需背景知識

EQ 題

超級市場自助角落是……

A　Self-serve corner

B　Self-served corner

C　Self-serving corner

D　Self-service corner

Self-control 是指……

A　一件物件的自我控制

B　一個人的自控能力

說某人充滿 self-interest，
是批評還是讚譽？

英文有一些前綴詞 (prefix)，加在其他的名詞、動詞或形容詞之前，便可創造新詞，例如：

(1) pre-　　pre-listening, pre-school, pre-suppose
(2) post-　post-exam, post-natal, postgraduate

這些前綴詞本身有其意思，例如 pre- 是「⋯⋯之前」，post- 是「⋯⋯之後」，故此不難猜到新詞的意思。

除了 pre- 和 post- 之外，以 self- 起首的英文詞語也很常見。可是，self- 並非前綴詞，隨意運用的話，很容易會鬧出笑話。舉例說，英文的 bag 可以用作動詞，解作把物品放進袋子中。但是，商店要求客人把付款後的貨品自行放入袋子中，可否說成 self-bagging？有超級市場曾經把供顧客自行包好物品的角落稱為 self-bagging corner，幸好沒多久便改掉，更正為 self-service bagging corner。大家知道問題出在哪裏嗎？原來 self-bagging 可解作自己把自己包起來！

不錯，self- 可以指人們自行去做某件事情，例如 self-reflection 是自我反思，在機場 self check-in 是自行辦理登機手續，self-drive 是自駕，self-study 是自學，a self-taught musician 是自學成材的音樂家等。那麼，餐廳或商店的自助角落，英文又怎樣說？曾經見過 self-serving corner 和 self-served counter 的寫法，可是兩個都不正確。

Self-serving 本義為心謀私利，例如一個謀取私利的政客是 a self-serving politician。至於 self-served 則應刪去 d，變

成 self-serve 作形容詞使用，即 self-serve corner 或 self-serve counter。Self-served 改為 self-service 也可以。

Self- 亦有另一個意思，解作「自身」，例如 self-actualization（自我實現）、self-pity（自憐）、self-respect（自尊）、self-righteous（自以為正直的）、self-esteem（自尊）、self-conscious（因在意自己的外貌或別人的看法而感到不自然），這些全部均與自身有關。

除了解作「自身」外，self- 還指物體自行活動，不須由人控制，例如 self-explode 的炸彈、有 self-timer 的相機、會 self-destruct 的無人偵察飛機等。

換句話說，「self ＋單詞」的合成義是甚麼，不能看作是文法規則便引伸出來，而只能基於每個單詞本身的意義，加上約定俗成，才能產生意義。故此，碰到一個陌生的 self- 詞語，猜錯其意思，絕不為奇。

即使詞典已收錄了部分以 self- 起首的英文詞語，也不一定可以望文生義。舉例說，self-made 的東西，是指人們自行製造、不假手於人，還是指在實驗室中自我誕生出來？一間 self-build 的房子，是指人們自行建造，還是像科幻片中自己變出來的那種？（註）沒有上文下理，有時單看 self- 字真會叫人想不透。

註：A self-made millionaire 是白手興家的百萬富翁；a self-build house 是自行策劃或親手建造的房子，這是相對於建造後才買賣的房屋。

近年流行 selfie 一詞，指自行為自己拍照，不假手於人，self- 在這裏解作自行去做某件事情。至於 -ie 在這裏只取其音，沒有實際意思。但英語也有用 -ie 結尾的詞語，用以解作「物體」，例如 goodies 是好東西、freebies 則是免費的東西。Selfie 一詞在 2013 年獲牛津詞典選為年度英文詞 (Word of the Year)。

17 用 the 與不用的取捨

自己想說甚麼而不是文法說甚麼

冠詞 (articles) 是英語學習的一大課題。從前讀中、小學時，我們都學過不少關於冠詞運用的規則，例如哪個名詞前加 the，哪個名詞前不用加。以下試舉數例：

✓	✗
(1) go to school	go to the school
(2) go to church	go to the church
(3) go to the park	go to park
(4) go to the market	go to market
(5) go to the post office	go to post office
(6) go to Repulse Bay	go to the Repulse Bay
(7) go to the Peak	go to Peak

另外，我們又要記着某些名詞前面一定要加上冠詞 the，例如 the sun、the moon、the sky；至於在文章中，首次提到 (first mention) 的人或事物用 a 或 an，第二次提到 (second mention) 時才能用 the。這樣的處理到今天仍然很普遍，以致部分人認為，冠詞運用純粹是語文形式 (language form) 的問題，只要熟讀這些形式上的法則便可。

今天我們對文法的認識大大提高了，以冠詞為例，運用時我們仍會注意其形式上的法則，例如我們會說 go to the City Hall 或 the Science Museum，但我們則只能說 go to Victoria Park 或 Stanley Market，而非 the Victoria Park 或 the Stanley Market。

但其實在選用哪個冠詞，或是決定是否選用冠詞時，有沒有更深層次的考慮？

就以下列四個句子為例，哪一句你覺得最自然：

(8) I am now in a park, and I can hear the bird sing.

(9) I am now in a park, and I can hear a bird sing.

(10) I am now in a park, and I can hear birds sing.

(11) I am now in a park, and I can hear the birds sing.

單從語言形式來看，上述四句均沒問題，但四個句子的意思和傳意效果，分別卻很大。一般情況下，第四句最自然，但 birds 只是第一次提到，說 the birds 豈非違反了所謂 first mention 和 second mention 的原則嗎？

其實我們一看句子 (11) 中的 the birds，我們的背景知識就告訴我們公園中有鳥兒，所以 the birds 指的是公園內的鳥兒，這是說話者和我們之間的共同理解 (shared understanding)，故此無須等待 second mention 才用定冠詞 the。

故此，冠詞的運用，絕不是單純的文法形式問題，而是往往取決於我們的想法，和溝通者之間的相互理解。說 The children go to school every day 時，school 代表概念而非一個特定的地方；同理，說教徒 go to church，church 表示的也是概念而不是地方。這解釋了為甚麼我們說上大學，英文是 go to university，而去 post office、market、library、supermarket 等地方時，名詞前面要加上 the，因為我們想着的是一個具代表性的地方，這些地方有其特殊的社會功能。

英文的冠詞不單純是形式問題，要把冠詞運用到得心應手不能僅靠熟讀文法規條，而是要通過大量的聆聽和閱讀，還要提高自己的文法智商。

以下句子正確嗎?

A   Police are looking for the suspect.

B   The police are looking for the suspect.

答案:A 和 B 都可以接受。A 的說法正日趨流行。

18 Whom 和 of which 會消失嗎？

文法傾向化繁為簡

EQ 題

以下的片語 / 句子可否成立？

the boy's legs
the tiger's legs
the table's legs
the chair's legs

the city's population
the population of the city

my computer's keyboard
the keyboard of my computer

I saw a house of which the windows were all broken.
I saw a house the windows of which were all broken.
I saw a house whose windows were all broken.

中文一概用「的」去表示文法中的所有格 (possessive)，例如「黃先生的新車」、「新車的門」，英文可以說 Mr Wong's new car，但 the new car's doors 又可否成立，抑或一定要說 the doors of the new car？下面的 possessive 's 的用法都可接受，你可以看得出一點脈絡嗎？

Jan's schoolbag	ladies' jeans
the school's policy	each other's friends
China's economy	cow's milk
yesterday's programmes	the rabbit's cage
the children's toys	

中小學英語課程處理 possessive 's 時，為了讓學生容易掌握，會把規律簡化，即凡擁有者是生命體 (animate)，用 possessive 's，即 Jan's schoolbag、the children's toys、ladies' jeans、cow's milk 和 the rabbit's cage；否則便要用「A of B」的結構，例如 the windows of the house、the floor of my room 和 the tone of his speech。但上面的其他例子顯示，某些非生命體的擁有者也可以用 possessive 's，其他的例子還有 the sun's rays、the ship's crew、the country's capital 等，究竟甚麼時候用 possessive 's，甚麼時候用「A of B」結構，可否歸納為較準確的文法規條？

生命體擁有者通常採用 possessive 's，所以說 Sam's wife、the donkey's legs、the horse's tail 沒有問題。但即使如此，有時候也有例外，譬如 chicken leg 和 fish head，當泛指某些食物時，便要略去 possessive 's。

可是，對於非生命體擁有者來說，甚麼時候可以用 possessive 's，這就難說得清楚了，例如 the legs of the table 可否改說 the table's legs？不說 the keyboard of my computer

而說 my computer's keyboard 是否也可以接受？the windows of his house 是否也可以說成 his house's windows？

原來哪些字可與 possessive 's 共用，沒有嚴謹的法則，很多時候只是約定俗成；故此，就算母語是英語的人士，遇到一些特殊的情況，也要停下來，想一想，再用直覺去判定可否用 possessive 's。

安全的說法當然是「A of B」，例如 the furniture of my office，為甚麼還要考慮可否用 possessive 's，即 my office's furniture？請比較下面兩句，假設兩句都成立，你會喜歡哪個說法？哪個說法較易組織？

(1a) He is looking at the upper left-hand corner of the computer screen.

(1b) He is looking at the computer screen's left-hand corner.

再看看相關的關係分句 (relative clause) 的例子：

(2a) I saw a bungalow the outer walls of which were all painted red.

(2b) I saw a bungalow whose outer walls were all painted red.

從概念是否容易明白，以至語言結構的難度來說，(1b) 和 (2b) (possessive 's) 都比 (1a) 和 (2a)（「A of B」結構）易明和較易組織；故此當人們遇上模稜兩可的情況，選擇 (1b) 和 (2b) 的說法仍是自然不過。這習慣在英文正有蔓延的趨勢，或許有一天 possessive 's 會全然取代「A of B」結構也說不定。

同樣，關係分句中的 whose 會否完全取代 of which？這情況並非全無可能，例如關係分句中的關係代名詞 whom，已經日漸為 who 所取代！

雖然目前 possessive 's 和 whose 分別可代替「A of B」結構 或 of which，但是後者較為嚴肅，例如下面各組的 b 句：

1a the White House's staff

1b the staff of the White House

2a This is a university whose students mainly come from other countries.

2b This is a university of which the students mainly come from other countries.

19 Suggest someone to do something 有甚麼問題？

動詞與句式的關係

EQ 題

1 He suggested her to see a doctor.

2 He suggested her see a doctor.

3 He suggested her seeing a doctor.

4 He suggested seeing a doctor.

5 He suggested that she sees a doctor.

6 He suggested that she saw a doctor.

7 He suggested that she should see a doctor.

8 He suggested that she see a doctor.

9 He suggested she see a doctor.

10 It was desirable that she see a doctor.

11 It was desirable that she should see a doctor.

12 It was desirable that she sees a doctor.

13 It was desirable she see a doctor.

不少學生在寫作時，會直覺地寫出 *I suggest him to go to the park，或 *He suggested her to see a doctor 等句子，也許出現得多，有時候連老師改作文時也動搖起來。上面兩個句子，正是當英語教師的舊學生，寄給我的兩個問題。

過度概括 (over-generalization) 文法規律，是外語學習者常犯的毛病，例如英文有以下這個句型：Subject ＋ Verb ＋ Object ＋ *to*-infinitive phrase，例句有：

Subject （主語）	Verb （動詞）	Object （賓語）	*to*-infinitive phrase （帶 *to* 的不定詞片語）
He	asked	me	to see the teacher.
I	wanted	the children	to go home.
She	told	her husband	to buy some groceries.

學生使用 suggest 時，也覺得可以說 He suggested her to see a doctor 等句子，而不知道有部分動詞，例如 suggest、recommend、insist 和 demand 等，不能放在上面的句式中使用。

先說最簡單的正確說法：He suggested seeing a doctor，suggest 後面用名詞片語，而 seeing 是動名詞 (gerund)，是名詞的一種，He suggested seeing a doctor 顯然沒有問題。但是如果要同時顯示 suggest 的受事者 (recipient)，如 her，便要用下面的說法：

(1) He suggested that she should see a doctor.

(2) He suggested that she see a doctor.

(3) He suggested she see a doctor.

(4) He suggested that she saw a doctor.

(5) He suggested she saw a doctor.

但 (2) 和 (3) 的 ... she see a doctor，有問題嗎？

(1) 用 should see 不難理解，就是類似 He said (that) she should see a doctor；(4) 和 (5) 的 saw 和 suggested 在時態上也配合，但 (2) 和 (3) 的 see，既非 sees 又非 saw，英文的分句 (clause) 中 she 和 see 怎能走在一起？

原來英文的表達方法有所謂「虛擬語氣」(subjunctive mood)，以表達說話者的一些願望，典型的用法是：

Subject	+	suggest demand insist stipulate require recommend	+	*that*-clause（that 分句）： • that 字可省去 • *that*-clause 中的動詞以基本形式 (base form) 出現

例如：

(6) The president has demanded that the union *end* the strike as soon as possible.

(7) The judge insisted that the defendant *be remanded* in custody immediately.

(8) I recommended that they *talk* to Mr Leung.

(9) She demanded the company *stop* sending her promotion emails.

總之，在 *that*-clause 中，無論主語是第一、第二或第三人稱，發生的時間是甚麼，動詞都是以基本形式出現。虛擬語氣亦在以下的句式中使用：

It is	+	important desirable essential vital imperative	+	*that*-clause

例如：

(10) It is important that you come to class punctually.

(11) It is imperative that she come to class punctually.

(12) It was essential that they come to class punctually.

最後，有兩點要補充。首先，以上兩句式都是較為嚴肅的説法。其次，上述提過的 recommend 的用法，即 I recommend that they talk to Mr Leung，在今天的英語世界裏，類似 I recommend them to talk to Mr Leung 的説法亦漸常見，雖然亦有不少人否定這説法，或只用於被動式，例如 Passengers are recommended to …。有趣的是，recommend 意義與 suggest 相近，但這種新興的説法應用到 suggest 這詞上，卻暫時未得到廣泛的接受，這又再反映，文法不是像代數或化學公式般工整。對於語言學習和工作者來説，語言觸覺還是至為重要的。

考考你

試重寫以下病句：

1 I suggested him to stay at home.

2 The law stipulates you to pay your income tax on time.

20 Disabled toilet 是怎樣的廁所？

如何解構複合詞？

Disabled toilet 可否解作
失效的廁所？

對於英文中的一些動詞，我們可以取其過去分詞 (past participle) 形式而作形容詞用，例如 an excited audience，excited（興奮的）來自動詞 excite 的過去分詞。其他的例子有 a broken glass、a frightened child、faded glory 和 interested parties。

Disable 也是動詞，to disable a computer 就是令電腦不能運作，變成 a disabled computer。那麼，a disabled toilet 是不是指不能運作的廁所？以此類推，married quarters 豈非應解作結了婚的宿舍，而不是已婚職員宿舍？Naked chat 是指網上交談本身是赤裸的？港鐵的 paid area 指該範圍已購了票？

原來 broken glass、frightened child、faded glory 等名詞片語，由「形容詞＋名詞」組成；而 disabled toilet、married quarters、naked chat 等看上去結構相同，但實際上是複合名詞 (compound noun)。

複合名詞由兩個或兩個以上的單詞組成，雖然其意義可以由單詞間的關係推敲出來，但這中間沒有嚴格的文法法則，很多時候是約定俗成。Married couple 是已結婚的一對，但 married quarters 之所以是 quarters for married staff，因為大家共同用這個說法。我們明白 naked chat 所指的是甚麼，是因為我們對某類人的上網行為有認識。我們知道 paid area 的意思，因為我們了解港鐵車站的設計。我們明白 disabled toilet 是供不良於行人士使用的洗手間，因為我們具備這樣的背景知識。

由於複合名詞的組成沒有固定的規律，有時候同一詞義有不同的呈現。教師培訓課程中，讓學員最感雀躍也最為擔憂的，通常是 teaching practice 這一環

節。Teaching practice 即教學實習，我們也可以倒過來說 practice teaching，意思跟 teaching practice 全無分別；教學實習還有其他叫法，如 student teaching、teaching practicum 等。正在受訓的教育系學生可稱為 teacher trainee，又可叫 trainee teacher，當然這並不表示複合名詞的成分字可以隨時倒過來，例如職前的教育系學生是 student teacher，但 teacher student 卻是指本身已成為教師而又在進修的學生。

複合名詞的意思，有時候不一定可以由字面看出來。如果大家第一次看見 no-brainer，也許會以為那是指一個無腦之人，可是 no-brainer 的實際意思，卻是指一件簡單容易、不須動腦筋便可解決的事情，例如：

John is a very smart person and this task is a no-brainer to him.

Dream catcher（或 dreamcatcher）不是一個浪漫的尋夢者，而是北美土著文化中的護身符，據說它能把所有惡夢捕捉起來，好使人們得以安睡。

有時候，是名詞片語還是複合名詞也得看語境，a walking stick（拐杖）是複合名詞，但在童話故事中卻可能是一枝會走動的棍條；an English teacher 是英籍教師還是英語教師，也只能看語境。在我的行業（英語教師培訓）裏，要準確地表達這個意思，會説 a teacher of English。

考考你

現時某些學校會邀請家長當義工，協助學校處理一些雜務，例如派發飯盒。大家知道「家長義工」的英文是 volunteer parent 還是 parent volunteer 嗎？

答案：parent volunteer

游賞文法的花園

21 為何 open 的相反是 closed 不是 close?

分清動詞抑或形容詞

詞典也説 close 是形容詞，
這裏用 close 有問題嗎？

香港人用英文說「開」、「關」時，經常犯錯，例如把 closed 寫成 close，又會說 *The library is opened from 10 a.m. to 8 p.m. 而不說 The library is open from 10 a.m. to 8 p.m.，這些錯誤例子存在了很多年，我們到今天仍然經常見到，不過 open 和 close 又的確很易混淆，少一點文法智商就會攪不清楚。

　　我們說商店、學校等機構的「開」(開門) 與「關」(關門)，可以是描述狀態，也可以是談論開關這動作。說狀態時，當然是採用形容詞而不是動詞，那麼 open 究竟是形容詞抑或是動詞？

　　湊巧地，open 既是形容詞，又是動詞。店鋪掛出正在開門營業的牌子時，表示營業中的狀態，牌子上所用的詞很少寫成 opened。可是人們在寫句子時，卻往往弄錯了詞性，用上了被動式動詞形態的 opened，例如：

(1)　*The museum is opened from Tuesday to Sunday.

(2)　*The library is opened from 10 a.m. to 8 p.m.

　　除非指的是 open 這動作，才有機會用到被動式動詞形態的 opened，例如：

(3)　The new library will be opened by the university president this Saturday.

　　相比之下，close 更易弄錯，close 同樣既是動詞也是形容詞，而作形容詞時，close 有兩個不同的意思呢！

　　首先，要表示商店關了門這狀態，當然要用形容詞，但正確的形容詞不是 close，而是 closed，這是因為形容詞 close 有另一解釋。Closed 指關閉的狀態，是由動詞 close 演變而成的形容詞，類似的單詞有 excited (源自動詞 excite)、frightened (源自動詞 frighten) 和 broken (源

自動詞 break）。正在開門是 open，正在關門卻是 closed，難怪人們容易混淆兩個詞。

Closed 的確是形容詞，但說兩人是很要好的朋友，卻不能説 *closed friends，應該使用形容詞 close 的本義，即 close friends。又例如：

(4) He is very close to his father.

(5) They live quite close to each other.

早前經過一家咖啡連鎖店，看見店鋪正在裝修，門前貼出告示，寫着 We will be reopen on the 18th of October。句子用了 will be，顯示寫句子的人將 reopen 看作形容詞。不錯，open 是英文固有的形容詞，但這是否代表 reopen 也可作為形容詞呢？這個問題可以有兩種看法：一，把 reopen 作為形容詞，因為它源自形容詞 open；二，reopen 不應作為形容詞，因為這不符合一般英文形容詞的構詞法。如果你運用文法智商，你的看法如何？

我的看法是，這則告示既然標明日期，並不是説單單在那天重開的狀態，而是説在十月十八日將會重開這行動，所以應該用動詞，即 We will reopen on the 18th of October，至於為甚麼不説 We will be reopened on the 18th of October，這裏牽涉到哪些動詞應在甚麼情況下使用主動形式，另文再談。

下面的句子中，斜體字是動詞抑或是形容詞？

1 The time has *come* for him to say goodbye to his family.
2 Thy kingdom *come*.
3 *Gone* are the days when we were so carefree.
4 Everyone has *gone* home.
5 The police have *closed* the area.
6 This is a *closed* area.

答案：動詞：1、4、5；形容詞：2、3、6

22 不像複數的複數名詞

複數名詞不一定有複數標記

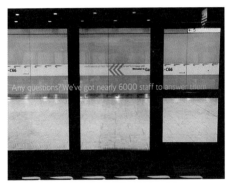

'Any questions? We've got nearly 6000 staff to answer them.'

這是倫敦希斯路機場的告示，寫着 6000 staff，數字是複數，但名詞 staff 看上去卻是單數，這是否犯了文法的錯誤？

我們都知道英文的 staff、team、audience 和 committee 等，都是集合名詞 (collective noun)，可以指整體，又可以指整體內的個別成員，例如：

(1) The team is very strong.
（team 作為整體）

(2) The team are having lunch now.
（team 作為個別成員）

(3) The committee consists of 12 members.
（committee 作為整體）

(4) The committee have discussed the matter for over four hours.
（committee 作為個別成員）

(5) The staff is well paid.
（staff 指整個工作團隊）

(6) The staff are well paid.
（staff 指工作人員）

傳統的文法書會提到，這些集合名詞如果與複數數字共用，例如 two staffs，指的是多於一個的工作團隊；two committees 是兩個委員會，不是兩個委員。若我們要說個別的工作人員，就得說 a staff member、a member of staff 或 three staff members 等。

可是，語言的用法會不斷改變，現今某些詞語的用法，可能已不再受固有的文法約束。若干年前，已有人開始在 staff 前面使用數字，以表示個別的工作人

員，漸漸人們開始接受 ten staff（十名員工）、twenty staff 等說法。如果要勉強解釋，可以說 ten staff 即 ten staff members，只不過 members 給省略了。但是我覺得這些後來的解釋並不需要，因為語言的改變並不一定會合乎傳統文法形式上的規條。

有趣的是，人們為甚麼會用 ten staff 指 ten staff members，而不跟隨傳統複數形式而說 ten staffs 呢？之前提到，傳統上，staff 的複數指多於一個的工作隊伍，這個意思還是偶爾要用到的，例如：

The company has two staffs working round the clock on the project.

於是人們指十位員工時，說 ten staff 而不說 ten staffs（十個工作隊伍），卻又巧妙地避免了出現混淆。

除了 staff 一詞外，police 一詞也出現類似的情況。從前，police 一般視作複數名詞，前面加 the 使用，例如 The police are still investigating the case；但到了今天，我們可隨意在 police 前加上數量詞 (numeral)，例如 several police、thirty police，或簡單的說 police，如 Police arrived at the crime scene in no time。但有趣的是，說一名警員時卻不可以說 a police 或 one police，而要說 a police officer 或 a policeman/policewoman。至於說整個警隊，則可以用單數概念的 the police force，或 the police department。

從以上的例子我們可以看到，個別詞語的用法可以有其獨特的法則，不受固有文法規管。說回篇首的相片，6000 staff 在今天是絕對可接受的說法。

23 小心以 s 結尾的名詞
真真假假的複數

'I have a good news to tell you.'

英文有複數標記 (plural marker)，但中文沒有，這為我們學習英文時帶來不少困擾。有一次，學生寫電郵給我，說 *I have a good news to tell you。我回覆時提醒他英文沒有 a good news 這種說法，他立即道歉，並自行將句子修正為 *I have a good new to tell you，我看後啼笑皆非，沒想到他會以為 news 是複數名詞！

　　事實上，news 是不可數名詞 (non-count noun)，沒有複數形式，只不過碰巧它的拼法以字母 s 結尾。另一個例子是 crossroads（交匯處），這個詞經常在片語 at a crossroads 中出現，意思是處於十字路口中，但不能因為它像單數名詞 (a crossroads) 而把 crossroads 改為 *crossroad，幸好類似的例子在英文並不多。那麼 headquarters（總部）的用法和 crossroads 是否相似？以下三個句子，哪一個是正確的？

(1) Their headquarter is in Central.
(2) Their headquarters is in Central.
(3) Their headquarters are in Central.

　　原來和 crossroads 一樣，headquarters 一定以 s 結尾，句 (1) 不可接受。句 (2) 和 (3) 都正確，動詞用 is 抑或 are 視乎把 headquarters 看成是單一的組織，還是其組成的各個建築物。

　　一般來說，英文只有可數名詞 (count noun) 才有複數形式，試比較以下兩組以複數形式寫成的名詞，大家有甚麼發現？

A		B	
clothes	noodles	books	mountains
headquarters	quarters（宿舍）	chairs	people
materials		children	

以上十個名詞，都是以複數形式寫成，但是大家有沒有發現，B 組的名詞可以和數量詞 (numerals) 一起使用，例如 ten chairs、sixty people、three mountains，但是 A 組的卻不能，我們不能以 *three clothes 來表示三件衣物，只能說 three pieces of clothing；兩碗麵不能說成 two noodles，除非在特殊情況下，例如在餐廳裏顧客和服務員都明白是指兩碗麵。我們可以說 We haven't got enough materials 或 We need more materials，卻不能說 I need two materials。Quarters 和 headquarters 都只能泛指宿舍和總部。

還要留意的是，clothes 的單數形式 cloth 指布匹，material 可以是不可數名詞，也可以是單數的可數名詞，例如 The curtain is made of a soft material。至於 noodles，一般採用複數形式，例如 I like instant noodles。Noodle 的單數形式也是可以接受的說法，例如 Instant noodle Is popular in Japan。

英文裏還有數個名詞，雖然也有單數形式，但一般會以複數形式使用，例如 congratulations、condolences、enquiries、apologies。恭喜別人時，要說 Congratulations 而不是 *Congratulation。同樣，表示哀悼時，我們要說 My condolences 而非 *My condolence。向人道歉，或表示不能出席會議時，也最好用複數的 apologies。商場或辦公大樓的詢問處，標示為 Enquiries 比 Enquiry 好。

文法歸文法，但當涉及個別詞語的用法 (usage) 時，卻不能夠一成不變的依足文法規條。

倘若遲了恭喜人家，事後補回，那是 to send someone a belated congratulation 還是 to send someone a belated congratulations？

答案：to send someone a belated congratulations

24 可以說 all-roundly 嗎？

副詞比你想像的多

All-roundly 是英文字嗎？

在〈應該説 travel happy 還是 travel happily？〉一文中，我提到數個看來像形容詞，但其實是副詞 (adverb) 的詞，包括 tight、direct、wrong、right、light。這些詞同樣可以加 -ly 作副詞使用，即 tightly、directly、wrongly、rightly、lightly。

除了上述幾個詞外，英文中還有一些不以 -ly 結尾的副詞，例如 fast、well、fine、alone、late 和 hard。學生一不小心，就會寫出 *I went to school lately、*She worked hardly 等病句，雖然 lately 和 hardly 確實存在，又碰巧都是副詞，不過意思卻與 late 和 hard 南轅北轍。

另一邊廂，英文中又有另一些詞語，看上去是副詞，但其實是形容詞來的，例如 lively、elderly、lovely、fatherly、stately、lonely、princely、miserly、motherly、leisurely、friendly，要小心不要被它們表面的拼寫騙倒啊！曾有朋友問，friendly 既然是形容詞，那麼「友善地」又應該怎樣説？可否説 They talked with each other friendlily？

在文法上，有所謂詞性 (word class)，傳統的叫法是 part of speech。英文的實詞 (lexical word)，不少都同時以名詞、動詞、形容詞和副詞的形式出現，例如：

名詞	動詞	形容詞	副詞
comfort	comfort	comfortable	comfortably
sadness	sadden	sad	sadly

我唸小學準備應考升中試時，便花了大量時間背誦數百個詞的各個詞性，還記得當時看見 beauty、beautiful 和 beautifully 沒有相關的動詞而感到奇怪。不過多年後發覺原來動詞 beautify 是存在的。

然而，語言和數學不同，沒有必然的齊整性。描述一個人孤獨地或友善地，甚或是傻氣地去做某件事情，這原本是很常遇到的情況，但偏偏英文卻沒有現成的 *lonelily、*friendlily（註）和 *sillily。要表達這些意思，唯有用較累贅的副詞片語 (adverb phrase)，例如 in a lonely way、in a friendly manner。

但語言是不斷轉變的，人們不是可以就着需要而創出新詞嗎？不錯，例如 sensitive（敏感）一向只是形容詞，但若干年前，有人創出 sensitize 這動詞，指令人對某事情敏感，當時就有不少英語為母語的人士，認為這個動詞既無需要，聽起來也怪怪的，而加以排斥；當然今天已沒有多少人會反對這個詞。

改變一個詞的詞性而創出來的新詞，能否為人接受，真是各有造化，以 all-roundly 為例，有一天成為英語標準詞也說不定，但暫時它還沒有這個資格呢。

最後一提，香港學生常常說 *I got to there at 10 o'clock 和 *He goes to home after school，其實 there 和 home 也是不像副詞的副詞，只須說 I got there at 10 o'clock 和 He goes home after school 便可以了。

註：曾經有詞典收錄 friendlily 一詞。我正在使用的 Microsoft Word 軟件，也沒有視之為錯字，但 friendlily 實際上很少人用，勉強使用有機會被當成是錯字。

伸延閱讀

想要知道英文除了名詞、動詞、形容詞和副詞外，還有哪些詞類，可參閱這個網站：http://www.oxforddictionaries.com/words/word-classes-or-parts-of-speech

游賞文法的花園

25 There is 和 There are 還有沒有分別？

口語與書面語之分日漸模糊

EQ 題

以下的句子是否成立？

There is one thing you need to remember.

There are a few things you need to remember.

There's a few things you need to remember.

There's a lot of people in the park.

There is a chair and a table in the room.

There are a chair and a table in the room.

在學校課程中，there is/are 是一個教師很重視的文法課題，學生要學會句子動詞如何和動詞後的名詞配合，例如：

(1) There is/was/has been a book on the table.

(2) There are/were/have been some books on the table.

這亦是熱門的考試題目。報章的英語問答專欄也經常教導讀者甚麼時候用 there is，甚麼時候用 there are。然而在日常英語運用中，真的是這樣嚴謹劃分的嗎？

在今天的口語裏，其實不難聽到下面的句子：

(3) There's a few things you need to remember.

(4) There's a lot of people in the park.

(5) There's twenty chairs in the room.

從文法上來說，這句式稱為 Existential-*there*，用以指出存在的人和事物，there 是因應文法需要而存在的主語，沒有實質的意思。這裏所牽涉的一致關係 (agreement) 和一般句子的「主語＋動詞的配合」(subject-verb agreement) 不同，在 He is a student 和 They are students 兩個句子中，動詞的選擇出現在主語之後，亦即看見主語是單數的 He，便採用單數動詞 is；看見主語是複數的 They，便採用複數動詞 are。

但是在 Existential-*there* 句式中，動詞的選擇要先於其後的名詞片語，正因如此，一些人對 There's 日漸取代 There are 的解釋，是因為人們在快速說話中，來不及想到目標名詞片語是單數還是複數，便要先決定動詞是單數的 is，抑或是複數的 are，於是採用較易的說法 There's，到發現目標名詞片語是複數時，除非把句子重頭再說一遍，否則便蒙混過關算了，經過習非成是，

今天很多人想也不想便說 There's 算了。

這樣的解釋不能否定，但也暫時沒有科學根據，所以另一個可能性便是約定俗成，有不少的人這樣說了，其他人也照說無誤。但是如果句子的名詞片語像下面的形式，那又應如何取捨呢？

(6) There is/are a chair and a table in this room.

這個例子取自 BBC 的 World Service 網頁 (http://www.bbc.co.uk/worldservice/learningenglish/grammar/learnit/learnitv128.shtml)。

如果我們根據傳統文法規則，a chair and a table 是複數，故此應說：

(7) There are a chair and a table in this room.

如果是追隨流行的說法，則是：

(8) There's a chair and a table in this room.

但網頁的答案只有一個，就是 (8) 的說法，並且提供了兩種解釋：

解釋一：There is a chair and a table ... 是 There is a chair 和 There is a table 的合併說法，這解釋令我想起代數公式 $a(b + c) = ab + ac$。

解釋二：Existential-*there* 句中動詞的選擇，取決於緊隨其後的第一個名詞是單數還是複數，既然 a chair 是單數，故此動詞便是 is，即 There's a chair and a table in this room.

其實 BBC 的解釋有點自圓其說，如果他們覺得大部分人會說 There's a chair and a table ...，就指出這現象好了。文法中的語言形式 (language form)，無須千年不變。

下面的説法是否存在（尤其於口語中）?

1　Here's some points to think about.

2　Here is a few tips for your travel plan.

3　Here's an envelope and some stamps.

答案：（答 There's a few/some/twenty … 一樣，此等説法都存在。

26 一個 so 字兩相宜

如何知道 so 是 so that 的意思？

EQ 題

試比較以下兩句：

A   I want to get fitter so I can join the swimming team.

B   I want to get fitter so that I can join the swimming team.

大家覺得哪一句可以接受，還是兩句都沒有問題？

我有一位舊學生在小學教英文，一天她和同事共同備課時起了爭拗。事緣六年級的課本中，有一課教 so 和 so that 的用法。教師用書提到學生經常混淆 so 和 so that，所以要向他們解釋兩者的分別。根據教師用書所載，我們用 so 來表示結果，用 so that 來表示目的 (We use *so* to show results, and *so that* to show purposes)。

我的舊學生在外國長大，判斷句子的對錯全憑直覺，所以上面的文法解釋讓她感到一頭霧水。不單如此，教科書上的例句也讓她覺得有問題：

(1) Footballers do a lot of exercise every day so that they can stay fit.

(2) Actors do a lot of rehearsals so that they can perform well.

她直覺覺得兩個句子中的 so that 改為 so 會更自然：

(3) Footballers do a lot of exercise every day so they can stay fit.

(4) Actors do a lot of rehearsals so they can perform well.

不過她的同事認為要跟從教科書的說明，於是雙方就此僵持不下。舊學生問我意見，我說教科書的解釋不算錯，so 一般用來帶出結果，例如：

(5) It was very cold outside so he stayed at home.

(6) She wants a new mobile phone so she saves up her spare money.

第 (5) 句和第 (6) 句的確只能用 so，不能用 so that，但是第 (1) 句和第 (2) 句中的 so that，卻可以改為 so，這種替換在口語中尤其常見，也即是說第 (3) 句和第 (4) 句沒有錯。

若是這樣，豈非 so 既可表示結果，又可表示目的？這樣會否帶來意義上的混淆？請比較下面兩組句子，看看哪組用 so 表示目的，哪組用 so 表示結果：

A	B
(7) I want to keep fit so I can join the marathon next year.	He has been exercising a lot in the last ten months so he can join the marathon now.
(8) She leaves home early each morning so she can catch the first bus.	She left home early so she arrived at the office on time.
(9) The teacher sent us the PPT file so we did not have to take notes.	The teacher sent us the PPT file so we did not take any notes.

很明顯，A 組句子中的 so 用作表示目的，B 組句子中的 so 則用來指出結果。由此可見，在實際應用時，so 的兩種用法甚少會帶來混淆。

想深一層，為甚麼 so 這個對等連接詞 (coordinating conjunction) 有兩種用法，但意思卻不一定會出現歧義？這個問題的關鍵，是句子中兩個分句在意義上的關聯。以上表中第 (7) 句為例，大家都知道，勤加操練的結果，就是可以參加難度高的比賽，例如馬拉松。至於第 (8) 句說早出門便能準時回到公司，因果關係則更明顯不過，不必多作解釋。

so 和 so that 可以表示不同意思，但有時候又可以交替使用。這再一次證明，文法不能當作純語言形式 (language form) 的規條。

27 為甚麼 look forward to 後必須用 -ing 形式？

文法背後的道理

EQ 題

以下哪個句子文法上有問題？

A   She likes dancing.

B   She likes to dance.

C   She enjoys to dance.

D   She looks forward to dance with Peter.

E   She looks forward to dancing with Peter.

F   She used to dance with Peter.

G   She is used to dance with Peter.

H   She is used to dancing with Peter.

I   She stopped to dance with Peter.

J   She stopped dancing with Peter.

以前有不少學生都不知道 look forward to 後面應接動名詞 (gerund) 而非不定詞 (infinitive)，例如：

(1) I look forward to see you next week.　　(✗)

(2) I look forward to seeing you next week.　(✓)

近年犯這個錯誤的學生似乎愈來愈少，可能由於老師千叮萬囑，look forward to 後面要用 -ing 形式的動詞，但如果我們明白背後的原因，而不把 look forward to 當作一個例外的情況，便很容易掌握其他例子。以下每一組句子中，哪一句正確，還是三句都正確？

(3a) I will return to think about it later.

(3b) I will return to thinking about it later.

(3c) I will return to this matter later.

(4a) He was very busy and didn't get round to check his mailbox.

(4b) He was very busy and didn't get round to checking his mailbox.

(4c) He was very busy and didn't get round to this matter.

(5a) We are committed to provide you with quality service.

(5b) We are committed to providing you with quality service.

(5c) We are committed to quality service.

在每一組句子中的 c 句，在 to 後面用了名詞片語 (this matter、quality service)。如果 c 句成立的話，則 b 句中的 -ing 片語 (thinking ...、checking ...、providing ...) 也應該成立，因 -ing 詞是可作動名詞 (gerund) 使用的。既然事實如此，三組中的 b、c 句都沒問題，但 (3a) 和 (5a) 為甚麼也成立？

這涉及要表達的意思，試比較 return 在 (3d) 和 (3e) 在意思上有甚麼分別：

(3d) I need to leave now. I will return to think about it later.（return 指「回來」）

(3e) I will now deal with the more urgent matters first. I will return to thinking about it later.（return 是「回到這事情」）

至於 committed，請比較：

(5a) We are committed to provide you with quality service.

(5d) We are keen to provide you with quality service.

(5e) We are determined to provide you quality service.

可以看出 committed 在 (5e) 的句型中乃回指主語 We 的形容詞，那麼，說 We are committed to provide you with quality service 或 We are committed to providing you with quality service，文法上兩者皆叫，在乎要表達的重點。

但 He didn't get round to checking his mailbox 的 get round to 卻只有一層意思，就是「去處理某事情」，和 look forward to 一樣，後面只能用名詞片語，即：

(6) I look forward to something. → I look forward to seeing you next week.

(7) He didn't get round to something. → He didn't get round to checking his mailbox.

其他的例子有：

(8) She enjoyed something. → She enjoyed reading.

(9) Tom is accustomed to something. → Tom is accustomed to taking a shower in the morning.

(10) Winnie is used to something. → Winnie is used to going to bed after midnight.

不過要留意的是，若單獨使用 used to，前面沒有 be，句子結構和意思會有所不同。試比較以下兩句：

(11a) Andrea is used to going to bed after midnight.

(11b) Andrea used to go to bed after midnight.

(11a)說的是習慣，而 (11b) 說的是往事。

同樣：

(12a) The students stopped their activity.

(12b) The students stopped to listen to the teacher.

(12c) The students stopped listening to the teacher.

若要在 (12a) 與 (12b) 兩個情況之中選擇，當老師的會希望看見哪個場景？不用説當然是 (12b)，因為那是指學生放下活動去聽老師説話。要是換成 (12c) 就不妙了，因為那是指學生不再聽老師的話！

28 千變萬化的條件句

究竟有多少類條件句？

Reservations

If you reserved iP xxxx in advance, please line up here.

圖中 reserved 應否改作 reserve 或 have
reserved？

以下三個條件句 (conditional sentences) 中，哪一句是談現在？哪一句是談過去？

(1) If I know the answer, I will tell you.

(2) If I knew the answer, I would tell you.

(3) If I had known the answer, I would have told you.

下面兩個條件句中的動詞搭配有沒有問題？

(4) If you *will step* over here, I *will give* you an application form.

(5) If you *should see* Peter, *tell* him I want to talk to him.

寫給學生看的文法參考書，一般提到條件句時，會將其分為三類，分別是：

Type 1: If I know the answer, I will tell you.

Type 2: If I knew the answer, I would tell you.

Type 3: If I had known the answer, I would have told you.

近年在一些文法書中，赫然發覺還有所謂 Type 0 的條件句，特色是兩個動詞均以簡單現在式的形態出現，例如：

(6) If you *heat* metal, it *expands*.

(7) If you *see* Joyce, please *ask* her to give me a call.

讀中學的時候，老師在課堂上花了很多時間，解釋在三類條件句中，動詞形式有甚麼不同的變化。例如在第一類 (Type 1) 條件句中，if 分句 (if-clause) 採用的動詞形態是簡單現在式，主要分句 (main clause) 的動詞形態是「will ＋動詞的原形」，例如 will tell。我和同學花了大量時間做相關的練習，務求充分掌握各類條件句中動詞的變化。

我想，現今的學生一定會被這些規條弄得頭昏腦脹，覺得英文文法是討厭的枷鎖。如果他們知道條件句在實際使用中更是千變萬化，他們會更加不知所措呢！

請看看下面例句中，條件分句和主要分句的形式：

(8) If you ordered a smart phone, please …

(9) If you start ow, you might get there on time.

(10) If you will step over here, I will give you an application form.

(11) If you should see Peter, tell him I want to talk to him.

(12) If I had applied to the course, we would be classmates today.

這些都不屬於三類基本的條件句，但是在實際的英語運用中卻經常遇到，然而學校多數不會教呢！再舉一例，文法書通常把第二類 (Type 2) 條件句解釋為純想像而與事實不符的現時情況，例如：

(13) If I knew the answer, I would tell you.（表示現時我並不知道答案）

(14) If the boss raised my salary, I would stay for another year.（表示上司不像會加薪）

其實當我們描述過去的事情時，也會用 Type 2 的條件句，講述有可能發生的事情，例如：

(15) She stayed in London all summer. At the weekend, if she had time, she would go to Hyde Park.

(16) Last year, he was posted to Japan. If he had business in Tokyo, he would usually stay at a friend's house.

(15) 和 (16) 形式是 Type 2，但意義上是 Type 1，即指有可能發生的事情，只不過語境是過去的事情。中文

表達條件的時候，往往要靠語氣和語境，而英文則只需要改變條件句中的動詞形態。

　　既然條件句這麼千變萬化，英語課程和參考書也不可能全部列出，那麼我們怎樣才能充分掌握條件句呢？我看還是要靠提高自己的文法智商，在日常聽和讀英文時，多留意、多思考。

伸延閱讀

Ron Cowan 引述了不少研究，指出很多中國籍的英語學習者，即使到了學士後階段，仍然掌握不好英語的條件句 (Cowan, Ron (2008). *The Teacher's Grammar of English*. Cambridge: Cambridge University Press, page 463)。

29 可否說 You're welcomed？

不要被字面意義所騙

櫃員服務設於本行地庫
歡迎所有客戶使用
Teller Service available
at basement level.
All customers are
welcomed.

在香港，人們經常混淆 welcome 和 welcomed 二字。
出現混淆的原因，是沒弄清楚 welcome 一詞的詞類。

到底 welcome 屬甚麼詞類？請讀一讀以下的句子，
判斷每句中 welcome 所屬的詞類：

A	B
(1) A: 'Thanks very much.' B: 'You're *welcome*.'	The prime minister was at the airport to *welcome* the visiting president.
(2) I had a wonderful time because the host made me feel *welcome*.	When she arrived at the school, she was *welcomed* by the principal at the school entrance.

從上述例子可以看出，welcome 既是形容詞（A 組句子）又是動詞（B 組句子）。也許由於「歡迎」一詞在中文較接近英文動詞的意思，以致 welcome 一詞在香港經常出現誤用的情況，例如歡迎外賣，英文不說 Takeaway is welcomed 而說 Takeaway orders are welcome，或簡化為 Takeaway welcome。

另一個涉及詞類誤用的例子，是經常出現在招聘廣告中的 commensurate。請大家看看以下例子：

(3) *Salary *will commensurate* with qualifications and work experience.

Commensurate 看上去有點像動詞，但其實是形容詞，故此上述句子應改為：

(4) Salary *will be commensurate* with qualifications and work experience.

看上去像動詞，其實是形容詞的例子還有 worth。將 worth 誤用作動詞的情況，在香港也頗常見，可能由於 worth 的意思接近動詞 cost。不錯，我們可以說

This handbag *costs* 5000 dollars，若想把 cost 改為 worth，則要說 This handbag *is worth* 5000 dollars。同理，右圖廣告中的 worths 應為 worth。

從另一個角度看，某些英文句式須配合某些詞類使用。香港中、小學生常犯的一個錯誤，就是不知 during 後面該用名詞還是名詞片語，因此會寫出類似以下句子：

(5) *During they were walking in the park, it started to rain.

另一個類似的例子是以下這個偶然在港鐵車廂中聽見的廣播：

(6) *Due to the next station is still being occupied, this train will experience a short delay.

某次，一隻狗走進港鐵範圍，我的朋友聽到以下廣播：

(7) *Due to an animal was found between Kowloon Tong station and Tai Wai station, trains will be slowed down.

要表達原因，英文還有 because、as、since 等連接詞 (conjunction) 可用，不一定要用 due to；須知 due to 乃介詞 (preposition)，後面只能用名詞片語 (noun phrase)，例如 due to the bad weather、due to the typhoon；而 the next station is being occupied 是分句，較難轉化成名詞片語；為免錯誤，乾脆用連接詞好了，例如：

(8) As the next station is still being occupied, this train will experience a short delay.

總括來說，寫英文句子時，要注意各個成分需要與甚麼詞類配合，以免句式出現錯誤。

英
文
秘
道

30 複數是指多於一還是指二或以上？

文法規條也沒有想清楚的事情

EQ 題

以下哪個說法可以接受？

A　One and a half day

B　One and a half days

C　One and a half year

D　One and a half years

E　A day and a half

F　A year and a half

在公函中經常看見 the followings 這個片語,例如:

In connection with your application, please note the followings:

如果緊接的句子列舉了數個項目,則出現這個錯誤的機會會更大,因為寫句子的人以為 following 是名詞,於是複數便是 the followings。但 following 並非名詞。這個片語其實是 the following items/matters/issues 等名詞片語的省略寫法,所以 following 後面不應加 s。

說回名詞的複數形式,我們都知道複數名詞要加上複數標記 (plural marker),例如一本書是 a book,兩本書是 two books,但倘若數量介乎一與二之間,又算是單數還是複數呢?我在臉書上作了一個小調查,問臉書朋友會選擇以下哪種說法:

A one and a half hour

B one and a half hours

結果選 A 的人超過半數。也有人認為要看對待文法的態度,例如按規範性文法 (prescriptive grammar),應說 one and a half hours;按描述性文法 (descriptive grammar),則應說 one and a half hour。

究竟英文文法中的複數形式,是指多於一,還是指從二開始的數量?我翻查了數本文法參考書,發現一個有趣的現象,就是文法書鮮有定義何謂單數 (singular)、何謂複數 (plural),彷彿大家都心中有數,不用明言。學校教單數和複數形式時,例子全都是整數,例如 one hour/two hours、one day/two days,於是說其他語言的英語學習者遇到介乎一與二之間的數量時,便只能靠自己判斷是否該在名詞加上複數標記。我在網上討論區看到

有不少人討論 one and a half 之後的名詞，該用單數還是複數形式，例如 one and a half hour/hours、one and a half day/days、one and a half week/weeks、one and a half month/months 等，看來這個問題困擾着不少英語學習者。

還有，不少英語是母語的人士，把複數定義為數量二及以上，但如果你直接問他們，應該說 one and a half hour 還是 one and a half hours 時，他們一般卻會說 one and a half hours。但正如某位網友所言，如果很多外語使用者都說 one and a half hour、one and a half week 等，那麼我們是否也應該接受這種說法？在英語作為全球語言的年代，這意見不無道理。其實在日常溝通時，大部分人也不會在意應該說 one and a half year 還是 one and a half years，但是一牽涉到評核就會出現問題。例如教師批改作文或文法練習時否定 one and a half hour 的用法，而家長則認為 one and a half hour 沒有不妥，這便會引起爭拗。

其實要避免上述的爭拗並非沒有方法，以後要用英文說 1.5 小時的時候，大家不妨改用 an hour and a half，而且這是很地道的英文說法呢！

考考你

下面的句子哪些是正確的？

A　One and a half hours is a long time to her.

B　One and a half hours are a long time to her.

C　An hour and a half is a long time to her.

D　An hour and a half are a long time to her.

答案：A 和 C

游賞文法的花園

125

探索思維的深處

31 介詞靠死記硬背？

先弄清楚要說甚麼

以前港鐵港島線的西面終點站是上環，列車快要到達上環站時，中文廣播會提示乘客這是港島線的終點站，並多謝乘客選乘港鐵。之後英文廣播會説：Thank you for travelling by MTR。但當我們離開車廂踏上月台時，卻看見指示板上寫着：Thank you for travelling on the MTR，究竟哪句才是對的？

老師在學校教授介詞 (preposition) 時，一般會將介詞和名詞或名詞片語配對起來，例如名詞 Monday，前面的介詞是 on，即 on Monday；名詞片語 Chinese New Year 前用 at 或 during，the train 前則用 on；但是説到乘火車作為交通方式時，則要説 by train，靠走路就是 on foot，彷彿介詞的用法是靠死記硬背的。這些概括的法則不能説不對，但在現實的英語運用中，應採用哪一個介詞，卻往往繫於傳意目的 (communicative intent)。

就文法而言，Thank you for travelling by MTR 和 Thank you for travelling on the MTR 兩者皆對，但當列車駛進終點站，要多謝乘客選乘港鐵時，哪種説法較切合當時的傳意目的？

搭乘飛機時，航班降落前，機長會對乘客説幾句話，譬如會感謝乘客選乘其航空公司。你認為下面哪一句比較合適呢？

(1) Thank you for travelling by plane.

(2) Thank you for flying in the air.

句子 (1) 就像 Thank you for travelling by MTR，重點在於如何由甲地前往乙地，句子 (2) 就像 Thank you for travelling on the MTR，重點在於 travel 的所在地。當然，我們都會記得，機長真正説的是 Thank you for travelling with ABC Airlines。當時的傳意目的，就是要感謝乘客選乘 ABC Airlines。

同理，列車快到終點站時，港鐵公司想感謝乘客選乘港鐵，而不是其他交通工具，最好的説法應該是甚麼，這就不言而喻了。

至於傳意目的如何影響説法，英國著名學者 Henry Widdowson 曾經用以下例子解釋：

（家中的電話在響）

    Wife: 'The phone is ringing.'

Husband: 'I'm in the bathroom.'

表面上，妻子好像是多此一説，丈夫的回應也看似無關，但妻子説 The phone is ringing 時，目的不在於描述電話的狀況，而是提醒丈夫要接聽電話，而丈夫説 I'm in the bathroom 時，目的也不在於指出他身在何處，而是解釋他為甚麼不能立即接聽電話。

英文有一些基本的句式，常用於表達某種傳意目的，例如：

(3) Could you (pass the salt), please?
（用於禮貌的請求）

(4) I'm not sure about that.
（婉轉地表示不同意）

(5) If I were you, ...
（用於提出建議）

但大部分這些話語中，其字面意義和傳意目的之間的關係，都不是一對一的，因而我們便不能立即看出話語的傳意目的。所以，在日常生活中培養自己的語言觸覺便至為重要。

說 by MTR 時，重點在於採用哪種交通工具；而說 on the MTR，重點則在於乘搭交通工具時所身處的地方。Thank you for travelling on the MTR 是多謝乘客在港鐵運輸系統上往來各處。如果想多謝乘客選乘港鐵，則應說 Thank you for travelling with the MTR。

32 In 和 on 的煩惱

思維決定採用哪個介詞

日本街頭的確有不少「趣怪」的英文告示，但這個在地鐵站內的告示是否有問題？要把 onto the train 改為 into the train 嗎？這背後牽涉到，我們應該說 on the train 還是 in the train 呢？

英文常用介詞 at、on、in 來指示位置，但要區分這三個詞之間的用法，實在令不少英語學習者感到頭痛。一方面，我們在中文沒有類似的細微劃分；另一方面，有關的文法規則並不十分明確。有人說 in the street，也有人說 on the street；而 in the playground 和 on the playground 的用法也是並駕齊驅。人們一時說 Please call me *on* 12345678，一時又會說 Please call me *at* 12345678。究竟介詞的應用有沒有法則可依？

最常聽到的法則，是說 at 指一個具體的點，on 指一個平面，in 則指一個空間，例如：

(1) He lives *at* 187 Long Street.

(2) He lives *on* Long Street.

(3) Long Street is *in* the old town.

不過實際應用起來，卻要考慮傳意重點，例如：

(4) Kitty is *at* the library.

(5) Kitty is *in* the library.

上述兩句均沒有問題，用 at 或 in 取決於說話的重心，看看以下兩組對話自有分曉：

Mary: 'Where is Kitty? I haven't seen her for hours.'

Peter: 'She's at the library.'

Mary: 'It's starting to rain. Kitty may get wet.'

Peter: 'Don't worry. She's in the library.'

再請大家讀以下兩句，猜猜哪一句告訴我們 Tom 是 ABC School 的學生？

(6) Tom is studying *at* ABC School.

(7) Tom is studying *in* ABC School.

由於 in 與空間有關，所以第 (7) 句的重點是 Tom 在 ABC School 的校舍內讀書。第 (6) 句用 at，有強調 Tom 在芸芸學校中於 ABC School 就讀的意思，也就是說 Tom 是這所學校的學生。因此，要告訴別人自己是某大學的學生，應說 I am a student at XXX University 而非 I am a student in XXX University。

除了傳意重點之外，另一考慮因素是，我們怎樣理解介詞後的名詞或名詞片語。一個電話號碼，究竟是代表一個點（電話號碼主人所在位置），還是線路呢？若是前者就用「at ＋電話號碼」，若是後者則用「on ＋電話號碼」。因為電話號碼不是實物，不同人有不同的概念，所以 at 與 on 兩者在現實英語中是並用的。

那麼實物的交通工具又如何？原來我們想到的巴士、單車、私家車、船、艇和飛機，跟以英語為母語的人想到的，概念上可能會有所不同。例如他們視 bus、bike、ship、train、plane 為一個平面，乘坐時是要「登上」(get on) 而非「走進」(get in/into)，故此他們說 get on a train/bus/bike/ship/plane，而他們視 taxi 和 car 為空間，故此說 get in/into a taxi/car。

細心的讀者會想到，boat 又如何？對了，英文所說的 boat 可大可小，故此除了說 on a boat 外，也可說 in a boat！

文初圖片中的 Don't rush onto the train，有沒有需要改成
Don't rush into the train 呢？

答案：如果 train 是取其一般火車的意思，Don't rush onto the train 是正
確的說法。但是 train 如果單看成是車廂這意思，則 Don't rush into
the train 亦可接受。

33 應該是 a discussion on 還是 a discussion of？

動詞後有沒有介詞反映思維

常聽別人說 a discussion on (an issue) 或 to discuss about (an issue)，但究竟 on 是否應改為 of？而說 to discuss about (an issue) 又有沒有問題？

很多人都弄不清 on 和 of 的用法，例如影評，英文是 a review on a film 還是 a review of a film？書本撮要是 a summary of a book 還是 a summary on a book？不錯，我們會說 a course on language awareness、a talk on road safety、a book on English pronunciation，那麼說 a discussion on human rights、a review on a film 不是順理成章嗎？

如果純以語言形式分析，要解答這問題並不困難。試比較下面兩組動詞片語：

A	B
(1) to review a book	to comment on a book
(2) to critique a paper	to lecture on a topic
(3) to discuss an issue	to reflect on an experience
(4) to investigate a case	to argue about an issue
(5) to summarize a chapter	to refer to a letter
(6) to explain the causes	to apply for a scholarship
(7) to evaluate a lesson	to reply to the boss

B 組採用了「動詞＋介詞＋名詞片語」的結構。若我們將這些動詞片語 (verb phrase) 轉換為名詞片語 (noun phrase)，原來的介詞 (preposition) 會全部保留：

to comment *on* a book	→	a comment *on* a book
to lecture *on* a topic	→	a lecture *on* a topic
to reflect *on* an experience	→	a reflection *on* an experience
to argue *about* an issue	→	an argument *about* an issue
to reference *to* a letter	→	reference *to* a letter
to apply *for* a scholarship	→	an application *for* a scholarship
to reply *to* the boss	→	a reply *to* the boss

A 組的動詞片語，用的是「動詞＋名詞片語」的結構，中間沒有介詞。奇妙的是，如果將這些動詞片語轉換為名詞片語，則全部都可以用 of：

to review a book	→	a review *of* a book
to critique a paper	→	a critique *of* a paper
to discuss an issue	→	a discussion *of* an issue
to investigate a case	→	an investigation *of* a case
to summarize a chapter	→	a summary *of* a chapter
to explain the causes	→	an explanation *of* the causes
to evaluate a lesson	→	an evaluation *of* a lesson

　　正因為有這樣的差別，所以較地道和準確的説法是 a discussion of … 和 a review of …。雖然在文法上，a discussion on 和 a review on 也不算錯。

　　但更深層次的問題是，上面 A、B 兩組動詞片語，在意思上有甚麼差別？A 組片語是「動詞＋名詞」，中間沒有介詞阻隔，動詞和名詞之間的關係緊密直接。説 to investigate a case，調查 (investigate) 甚麼？就是案件 (case)；説 to evaluate a lesson，評核 (evaluate) 甚麼？就是一堂課 (a lesson)。B 組片語是「動詞＋介詞＋名詞」，中間多了一個介詞，名詞作為動詞的受事者 (recipient) 這關係便沒有那麼直接和緊密了。to lecture on a topic 就是就一個題目進行演講；to reflect on an experience 就是就一段經歷作反思。

　　最後要補充的是，如果一個動詞同時適用於 A、B 兩組的結構，例如 to report an incident 和 to report on an incident，那麼也會同時有兩種轉換為名詞片語的方法。故此既有 a report of …，亦有 a report on …。

除 a discussion of something 外，英文的確有 a discussion about something 的説法，和 a discussion of something 在意思上有分別。雖然我們可説 a discussion about something，但 *to discuss about something 卻不可接受，因 discuss 是及物動詞 (transitive verb)。

34 為甚麼説 in the building 卻要説 on the premises？

不要完全依賴翻譯詞

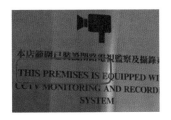

Premises 的正確用法是甚麼？

在香港，建築物範圍內張貼的告示，經常會出現 in this premise。此一片語的問題有二：首先，雖然 premise 一詞確實存在，但指建築物時，只可以使用複數形式的 premises；其次，premises 對應的介詞是 on 而非 in，所以正確的說法是 on these premises。那麼，為甚麼我們將 premises 改作 building 時，會說 in this building 而非 on this building 呢？On the street/playground 和 in the street/playground 哪個說法正確？

試比較下面兩組和地方有關的名詞：

A		B	
garden	restaurant	premises	farm
library		estate	

與這些英語單詞對應的中文詞語，所表達的都是指某種空間，因此我們說 in the garden、in the library 之餘，也很自然的會說 in the estate、in these premises 等。但原來 premises、estate 和 farm 三個詞，在英語世界裏的定義是一個平面而非空間。以 farm 為例，《牛津高階英漢雙解詞典》提供的定義為：

an area of land, and the buildings on it, used for growing crops and/or keeping animals

這定義的重點在於 an area of land。同樣，estate 的定義也是與平面的土地相關：

an area of land with a lot of houses or factories of the same type on it

Premises 也有類似的意思，這就解釋了為甚麼我們說 in the garden、in the house、in the restaurant，但卻要說 on these premises、on the housing estate 和 on the farm 了。

這種對地方在概念上的差異，解釋了為甚麼有人說 in the playground 和 in the street，也有人會說 on the playground 和 on the street。不錯，這兩種說法可以解釋為英式英語和美式英語的分別，但其實當中亦涉及到我們怎樣理解 playground 和 street 的意思。如果我們把 playground 和 street 想像為一個進行各式活動的空間，我們便會說 in the playground 和 in the street，但如果我們把這兩個地方視作平面，則會說 on the playground 和 on the street。

再以 field 為例，如果大家視之為空間，便會說 The children are playing in the field，如果視之為平面，則會說 The children are playing on the field。

上面提到，要說 in the street 還是 on the street，取決於我們怎樣想像 street 這個地方。現在讓我們來做個實驗，請大家想像一下 road 這個詞，看看到底腦海中出現的是平面還是空間？

一般人想到 road 都會想起平面，因此少有人爭論應該說 in the road 還是 on the road，大家都會自然地說 on the road。

當出現新鮮事物時，在概念上的分別更易從介詞體現出來。例如你會說 in a space station 還是 on a space station？談到虛擬世界裏的 website、the Internet、blog 等意念時，究竟它們是空間還是平面，很多時都只能依靠大家的共同理解。例如大多數人都會說 on your website、on the Internet、on his/her blog，但一說到 post 和 email，介詞則自動換成 in，例如 in your post 和 in your email。

35 誰決定名詞可數與不可數？

概念決定名詞的可數性

英文名詞，部分是可數名詞 (count noun/countable noun)，部分是不可數 (non-count noun/uncountable noun)。可是英文名詞的可數性 (countability)，卻從來都不是一成不變的，會隨着使用而改變。

　　舉例說，tea、coffee、coke 等不可數名詞，在日常生活中可以量化成 two teas、three coffees、four cokes 等；不過，五個麵包卻不可以說成 five breads。在餐廳說要 a coffee 時，說和聽的人都明白所指的是咖啡沖製完成端出來給客人的形態，即是說，是一杯一杯的。但英文 bread

只是指用麵粉烤焗而成的食品，它不是指個別的麵包製成品。麵包製成品可以是一個一個，也可以是一塊一塊的，英文有 roll、bagel、bun 等詞指個別的麵包製成品，說一塊一塊的麵包時，便要說 a piece of bread 了。

　　一個名詞的可數性來自其意義，但是這意義卻可以隨着時間而演化。於是，一個原本是 non-count 的名詞，可以由於社會中使用上的需要，而變為 count noun。二十多年前還未有電子郵件的年代，mail 泛指郵件，個別的郵品是 letter、postcard 和 parcel，要說三件郵品，必須說 three pieces of mail，不能說 *three mails。當電郵初出現時，電郵 (electronic mail) 仍然是泛指電子郵件，屬

於 non-count 名詞。當年有一齣很受歡迎的電影，片名叫 You've got mail，說的雖是電郵，但英文仍是 You've got mail，不是 *You've got mails。

當年，我們提及一封電郵時，必須說 an email message；隨着電郵的迅速興起，每次都說 an email message、some email messages 讓人感到有點不耐煩，於是有人開始把 email 當作 count noun 來使用，an email、five emails 等說法應運而生。

但是起初並非所有人都接受這種用法。我手上還有一封由某政府部門的高層官員發給某中級官員的備忘 (memo)，指責他在公文中說 an email 而不是 an email message。今天重看這封備忘，簡直不能相信曾經有官員因說 an email 而被上級訓斥。

然而，沒有人可以阻擋語言的演變，隨着電郵的廣泛使用，這個詞經歷了這個轉變：

electronic mail (non-count) → E-mail → e-mail → email (non-count) ＋ an email (count)

這不單是寫法的轉變，而在概念上，electronic mail 由泛指電子郵件，添加了「一封一封」的意思，以至今天我們可以隨便說 I have replied to ten emails already。當然，email 作為 non-count noun 的用法仍然存在，例如說 Answering email is time-consuming。

另一個例子是 software，這個詞原本泛指軟件，詞典仍然把它標示為 non-count noun。但今天你仍會堅持說 a piece of software 或 a software programme 嗎？抑或你可以接受 a software、these softwares 等說法？

很多英文名詞都能同時作為 count noun 或 non-count noun 使用，例如：change（改變）、reflection（反思）、thought（思想）、life（生命）、communication（溝通）、revision（修正）、exploration（發掘）、pleasure（快慰）、observation（觀察）等等。你還想到其他的例子嗎？

36 為何於校名中冠以The可增加氣勢？

不要把冠詞看作單純文法問題

這些大學的官方名字是甚麼？

香港大學於一九一一年成立，是香港當時唯一一所大學，所以大學的英文名稱，就順理成章的寫成 The University of Hong Kong。到了一九六三年，中文大學成立，以發揚中國文化為辦學宗旨之一，故此大學定名為 The Chinese University of Hong Kong。一九九一年，香港成立第三所大學，即香港科技大學，該校致力於科技研究，如果創立科技大學時，大家能為院校取英文名字，你會選擇以下哪一個？

(1) The Science and Technology University of Hong Kong

(2) The University of Science and Technology of Hong Kong

(3) The Hong Kong University of Science and Technology

(4) Hong Kong University of Science and Technology

第一個名字的結構和中文大學的英文名字相同；第二個名字的結構，源自澳洲一些科技大學的名字；第四個名字的結構，跟香港浸會大學（Hong Kong Baptist University）的名字相同。論結構，四個名字均屬正確無誤，可是論氣勢，還是第三個名字 The Hong Kong University of Science and Technology 最好，大家知道為甚麼嗎？

冠詞 the 的其中一個用法，是指出事物乃獨一無二，最耳熟能詳的例子有 the sun、the moon、the universe、the east、the west、the Earth，以及 the Pope（教宗）。除此以外，定冠詞（definite article）還可以指社會上有特殊地位而為大家熟悉的人和事，例如 the Queen（英女皇）。誠然，現今世界並非只有一位女皇，但在英國說 the Queen 就一定是指英女皇。同理，在香港說 the Peak 就一定是指太平山頂，不會是大帽山山頂。

上面提到 the 所具備的兩個特點，清楚顯示在以下的對話中：

John: 'Hey, I just saw David Beckham a minute ago!'

Jill: 'You mean *the* David Beckham?'

有不少大學以地名命名，例如國內有 Zhongshan University、Shenzhen University、Peking University；英國有 Durham University 和 Newcastle University；澳洲則有 Victoria University 和 Queensland University of Technology。香港科技大學的名字，理論上可以跟 Queensland University of Technology 一樣，定為 Hong Kong University of Science and Technology，以 Hong Kong 純粹顯示大學的地理位置，但是在名字前面加了冠詞 The，聽起來便有獨一無二的感覺。著名的紐約城市大學，英文名字是 The City University of New York，以突顯其特殊地位。香港浸會大學，理論上也可以在英文名字前加上 The，當然大學是否要塑造獨特的感覺，是另一種考慮。

除了大學名字外，其他地方的名字也有類似的考慮。如果純粹是一個名字，則說 Hong Kong Park、Ocean Park 便可。香港只有一所動植物公園，故而是 The Hong Kong Botanical and Zoological Gardens。香港的博物館，例如 Hong Kong Science Museum 和 Hong Kong Museum of History，全都沒有冠以冠詞 The，為甚麼不像 The British Museum（大英博物館）般冠以 The？想想它們的規模和國際知名度，便明白了。

以下學府的官方名稱中，哪個包含冠詞 The？

1 City University of Hong Kong
2 Hong Kong Polytechnic University
3 Hong Kong Institute of Education

37 Would you marry me 是求婚嗎？

英文表示假設的方法

EQ 題

甲和乙是很熟稔的同事，他們正在辦公室外小休。甲想抽煙，他應該跟乙說以下哪一句呢？

A   Would you mind if I smoked?

B   Do you mind if I smoke?

這樣算求婚嗎？

有一次到一間中學向高年級的學生演講，題目是「中英溝通方法的一些異同」，我請在座的男學生想像，有一天用英語向心儀對象求婚時，應該說以下哪一句：

(1) Will you marry me?

(2) Would you marry me?

大部分同學憑直覺選擇了前者，而這也是正確的答案。那麼，後者是出了些甚麼問題呢？

很多人將 would 視為 will 的過去形態使用，在說到過去的事情時，他們會把 will 改為 would，例如：

(3) He said he would do it.（比較 He said, 'I will do it.'）

(4) She told me she would pay me back.

(5) I was hoping you would join us.

其實大部分時間，would 都是用於講述現在或將來發生的事情。would 和 will 的分別，在於 would 表達假設，試比較以下兩句：

(6) If she works hard, she will pass the exam.

(7) If she worked hard, she would pass the exam.

第 (6) 句用現在式配「will＋動詞」的結構，表示事情有機會發生。第 (7) 句用過去式配「would＋動詞」的

結構，代表純粹的假設，暗示事情沒甚麼機會會發生。
這也解釋了為何在「wish ＋分句」的結構中，分句採用
will 而非 would，因為這個句型表達的是慨嘆而非期望，
例如：

(8) I wish you will listen to me.　(✗)

(9) I wish you would listen to me. (✓)

由於 would 表示假設，所以常用作客氣請求，例如：

(10) I will be grateful if you can reply to this letter at your
early convenience.

(11) I would be grateful if you could reply to this letter at
your early convenience.

以上兩句的文法均正確，但第 (11) 句用了表示假設
的 would，語調更加客氣。將第 (11) 句翻譯成中文，意
思是「本人明白閣下事務繁忙，但假若閣下能在百忙中抽
時間盡早回覆，本人將感激不已」。

不過，這種客氣請求要看對象，若是朋友之間過分
客氣會顯得見外。例如甲和乙十分熟稔，甲若想問乙是
否介意他抽煙，宜用 Do you mind if I smoke? 甚至只說
Mind if I smoke?。若說 Would you mind if I smoked?，恐怕
顯得過於客氣，不太自然。

再舉一例，在舞會中若想邀請別人共舞，應該說以
下哪一句？

(12) Do you like to dance?

(13) Would you like to dance?

答案視乎二人之間有多熟絡。較安全的問法是
Would you like to dance?，但別人可能會覺得你過分客氣，
反而想與你保持距離。

探索思維的深處

155

英文還有一些典型的句式用來表示假設，例如：

(14) If only it would rain.
(要是下雨就好了。)

(15) It would be crazy to reject such an offer.
(傻子才會拒絕這個建議。)

(16) Would that you were here!
(但願你也在這裡！)

回到文章起首的話題。文法上，Will you marry me? 和 Would you marry me? 均是正確，但正如剛才所解釋，would 有假設意味，在求婚時若還這樣客氣，好像顯示求婚者沒有多大信心，這樣子聽的人應該也不會太興奮吧？

知多一點點

時至今日，偶爾還會有人寫 I/We should be grateful if you could ...，但已沒有多少人會因應主語 We 而決定用 should 還是 would 了。

38 用 It is because 最安全？

善用不同句式去表達重點

EQ 題

Why do you often stay at home at the weekend?
要回答這個問題，你會選擇以下哪個答案？

A It is because there are many people in the streets.

B This is because there are many people in the streets.

C I stay at home at the weekend because there are many people in the streets.

D It is because there are many people in the streets that I often stay at home at the weekend.

E Because there are many people in the streets.

F Well, there are many people in the streets.

在以上六個答案中，大家覺得哪個答覆有文法問題？哪個答覆最自然？

回答閱讀理解練習中以 Why 一詞提出的問題時，是否需要以 It is because 起首？前陣子跟一位當教師的外籍朋友聊起這個話題，他說香港學生喜歡用 It is because 來開句，他舉了以下例子：

(1) At the weekend, I usually stay at home. I don't like to go out. It is because there are too many people in the streets.

朋友說，他最討厭學生這樣寫作，但凡見到以 It is because 起首的句子，一律扣分。那麼，是否凡以 It is because 起首的句子，都有問題？

英文最常出現的三個基本句型，分別是：

（一）主語 ＋ 動詞
　　例：John is sleeping.

（二）主語 ＋ 動詞 ＋ 賓語
　　例：John killed Mary.

（三）主語 ＋ 動詞 ＋ 補語 (complement)
　　例：John looks tired.

採用基本句型固然是穩打穩紮的做法，但有時候若採用一些較不常用的句型，可以帶出特別的效果。以下三句所要表達的意思相同，但效果卻不一樣：

(2) John killed Mary.

(3) Mary was killed by John.

(4) It was John who killed Mary.

現在請選其中一句，以完成 Peter 和 Paul 的對話：

Peter: 'I heard that Sam killed his girlfriend Mary.'

Paul: 'Oh, that's not true ...'

句 (4) 是最適切的說法。句 (2) 和 (3) 不能說是錯，但是要用特別的語氣補救，才能令人聽得明白。第 (4)

句強調凶手是 John 而非別人。文法上第 (4) 句稱為分裂句 (cleft sentence)，通常是說話時想加以強調某件事情，或否定先前的另一說法時採用的。

同理，It is because there are too many people in the streets 不是句式有誤，而是在沒有特殊需要的情況下使用 It is because，可能會引起誤解。像 It was John who killed Mary 一樣，我們可以用 It is because 來否定別人先前提出的理由，例如：

A: 'You don't often go out at the weekend. You must have a lot of work to finish at home.'

B: 'Oh, it's not because of that. It's because there are too many people in the streets.'

It is because 的另外一個用法，是加以強調事情的理由，句式一般會和 if 字連用。已故著名德國作家 Herman Hesse 有一句名言：'If I know what love is, it is because of you'，我們可以想像到聽到這句話的人 (即句子中的 you) 是何等興奮。試細讀以下兩句，感受一下句子在傳意效果上的差異：

(5) I know what love is because of you.

(6) If I know what love is, it is because of you.

It is because 也可以配合 that 使用，以達到強調理由的效果。試比較以下三句：

(7) I am always nagging at you because I care about you.

(8) Because I love you, I need to tell you the truth.

(9) It is because I love you that I need to tell you the truth.

第 (7) 句是純粹的敘事，第 (8) 句突出理由，但論強調的程度，第 (8) 句顯然仍不及第 (9) 句。

至於回答閱讀理解中以 Why 提出的問題，其實只要把正確的理由直接了當地說出來，便可以了。

39 時態非時間

tense 並不等同 time

他們不願再 apologize 嗎？

我們學習英文的時態時，往往將各種時態和時段對應起來，例如：

時段　　時態

過去　→　過去式 (past tense)

現在　→　現在式 (present tense)

將來　→　將來式 (future tense)

但請看看以下句子採用的時態，以及和事情發生時間之間的關係：

(1) She has seen the film already.（has seen 是現在式的一種，但她可能是六個月前看這套電影的啊！）

(2) Boys will be boys.（will be 是將來式，但難道這些男孩現在不是男孩？）

(3) 報紙新聞標題：Man dies after being shot in the head（該人已死去，還用現在式？）

由以上的例子，可見時態的運用，和事情發生的真實時間，沒有必然關係。的確，當傳意目的是純粹描述時，我們選用的時態是會配合事情發生的真實時間，例如採用過去式去描述已發生的事情；但除此之外，還有其他因素會影響我們對時態的選擇。例如下面兩組對話中，Peter 的哪個回應比較自然？

對話一

John: 'Hey, Peter. Shall we go to see that film together?'
Peter: 'Well, I have seen it three times.'

對話二

John: 'Hey, Peter. Shall we go to see that film together?'
Peter: 'Well, I saw it three times.'

直覺告訴我們，I have seen it three times 較為妥貼，但 Peter 看電影這事實，明明發生在過去，為甚麼 Peter 卻應採用現在式這一種，即現在完成式 (present perfect tense) 的 have seen 去回答 John 的問題呢？要明白箇中道理，先要理解英文時態的本義。

　　雖然我們常說「時態」，但其實英文文法中的「時」和「態」，是兩個不同的概念。從動詞形式的角度看，英文中只有兩個「時」(tense)，分別是「過去」(past) 和「非過去」(non-past)，分別用以標示 past tense（如 finished、climbed、applied）和 present tense（如 finish、climb、apply）。

　　英文的「態」(aspect) 則用於反映我們如何理解及表述事情本身。「態」分為兩種，分別是「進行」(progressive) 和「完成」(perfective)；前者用於表示事物正在進行，後者則強調完成。「時」和「態」雙劍合璧，就構成我們熟悉的各個時態，如現在進行式、過在完成式等。

　　以現在完成式 (present perfect) 為例，如果所描述的事情發生在過去，但說話者採用現在完成式，那麼，說話的重點便側重於事情和現時 (present) 相關，兼且已經發生了 (perfective)。

　　在 John 和 Peter 的對話中，John 請 Peter 看某齣電影，Peter 要推卻他，如果 Peter 用純報導的簡單過去式 (simple present) 回答，便顯得答案與現在無關，John 聽了可能會摸不著頭腦。

　　相反，文初的告示中用了純報導的 apologized，給人的感覺是道歉與現況之間沒有關連，會令人覺得這道歉來得沒有誠意。

40 I love reading 和 I love to read 沒有分別？

如何決定用不定式還是動名詞

英文有一些動詞，例如 begin、start、continue、like、love、hate，其後面可以同時以不定式 (infinitive)（即 to ＋動詞基本形式）和動名詞 (gerund)（即動詞的 -ing 形式），作為它們的補語 (complement)，但這是否表示兩種用法可隨意交換？先請大家憑直覺判斷以下每組的兩個句子有沒有分別：

(1a)　It started to rain.

(1b)　It started raining.

(2a)　He continued to read.

(2b)　He continued reading.

(3a)　Do you like to dance?

(3b)　Do you like dancing?

　　這問題不易討論，就以 (3a) 和 (3b) 而言，學者 Bolitho 和 Tomlinson（註 1）認為這兩句在意思上沒有分別，只是後者在美式英語中較為常見。我在網上英語學習討論區，也看過一些英語是母語的人士，認為 Do you like to dance? 和 Do you like dancing? 沒有分別。

　　但是如果我們再看看以下的兩段對話，直覺上你會否覺得，B 的兩個可能回應之中，其中一個較好？

對話一

A: 'What do you do in your spare time?'

B: 'I like reading/like to read.'

對話二

A: 'There's still an hour before the plane takes off. Do you want to take a nap now?'

B: 'Well, I like to read/like reading.'

學者 George Yule（註2）指出，很多動詞在句子中同時可以使用不定式（如 to dance、to cook、to swim）或動名詞（如 dancing、cooking 、swimming），但意思上，有以下的分別：

不定式 (to dance/cook/swim)	動名詞 (dancing/cooking/swimming)
較像動詞	較像名詞
傾向指行動	傾向指事件
誰是主事者較明確	主事者不一定清晰
有可能發生	會發生或已發生

Yule 以 I like dancing 為例，指出説話者可能只是喜歡舞蹈，他自己卻可能不會跳舞；相反，説 I like to dance 的人，是表示自己喜歡去跳舞。

所以，It started to rain 和 It started raining 還是有分別的。説 It started to rain，重點在於開始的那一刻；説 It started raining，重點是下雨這一事件，而且可能是預料之內，更有可能會延續一段時間。

經過 Yule 的解釋，我們也許明白，在以下一段話語中，為甚麼以 It started to rain 作結，比用 It started raining 較為妥貼：

The weather had been fine for several days. Yesterday, Mr Chan decided to take his children to the Peak. But just when they were about to leave home, it started (to rain/raining).

同理，He continued to read 較着重他繼續去看書這個決定和行動，説 He continued reading 則隱含他一直在看書，而他繼續這狀態。

當然，我們日常說話，很多時不需要十足精準，用不定式或動名詞不會構成嚴重誤解，但要達到超卓的語文水平，這些細微的分別正是表現功力的地方。而學校如果教授文法時，只着重語言形式 (language form)，例如不定式結構和動名詞結構的互相轉換，而忽略文法規律背後的意思及傳意效果，則學生只懂在文法練習上繞圈，而不能從而提高說和寫的水平。

註1：Bolitho, Rod and Tomlinson, Brian (1995). *Discover English* (New Edition). Oxford: Heinemann, page 90.

註2：Yule, George (1998). *Explaining English Grammar*. Oxford: Oxford University Press, page 220.

考考你

試重看本文中兩段對話，你認為 B 的回應哪一個較為妥貼？

答案：對話一：I like reading.
對話二：I like to read.

走出邏輯的迷宮

41 為甚麼不能說 reply me？

兩個字的距離真的反映意義上的距離

EQ 題

請圈選你認為正確的句子。

A   Please reply me at your earliest convenience.

B   Please reply to me at your earliest convenience.

C   Please answer me at your earliest convenience.

D   Please answer to me at your earliest convenience.

男士對女朋友說晚上致電給她，以下哪個說法最為溫馨？

A   I'll call you tonight.

B   I'll give you a call tonight.

C   I'll give a call to you tonight.

每天收到的電郵中，間或有些問題要請我回覆。這些郵件中，有些會寫 *Please reply me。*Please reply me 這個錯誤可能是寫郵件的人，將中文的「請覆我」直譯成英語所導致，其實英文要說成 Please reply to me。

英文的動詞可分為及物動詞 (transitive verb) 和不及物動詞 (intransitive verb) 兩大類。如果不及物動詞後面要跟賓語 (object)，我們需要在動詞後面加上介詞 (preposition)，例如：

(1) They laughed the boy.　　　(✗)

(2) They laughed *at* the boy.　　(✓)

(3) I like listening music.　　　(✗)

(4) I like listening *to* music.　　(✓)

有些接上賓語的動詞，後面可以加介詞，但不加也無妨。試比較 A、B 組在意義上的分別：

A	B
(5) He kicked the cat.	He kicked at the cat.
(6) I shot the bird.	I shot at the bird.
(7) Peter flew the plane.	Peter flew in the plane.
(8) She hit me.	She hit at me.

兩組句子在意義上的最大分別，在於 A 組句子中的賓語直接受動詞的動作影響，而 B 組句子中的賓語，影響則沒有那麼直接。譬如說 He kicked the cat，表示貓被踢中了，但若說 He kicked at the cat，我們則只知道男子舉腳踢，至於有否踢中貓則不得而知。說 Peter flew the plane，我們知道飛機由 Peter 駕駛，但若說 Peter flew in the plane，我們只能確定飛機上有 Peter 這位乘客，至於是否由他駕駛飛機則無從得知。

為甚麼動詞與賓語之間，有沒有介詞會產生意義上的分別？這和語言學裏的語言距離 (linguistic distance) 和概念距離 (conceptual distance) 有關。一般情況下，句子中的成分（如主語、動詞、賓語、狀語等）愈接近，意義上的關係愈密切。在 A 組句子中，賓語和動詞中間全無阻隔，而在 B 組句子中，賓語和動詞之間則多了個介詞，這造成了意思上的分別。

上述的分別在包含直接賓語 (direct object) 和間接賓語 (indirect object) 的句子中也會看到。以下是英文教學中常見的句子轉換練習：

(9) She made them a cake.
→ She made a cake for them.

(10) He got her some flowers.
→ He got some flowers for her.

(11) They sent me a postcard.
→ They sent a postcard to me.

不要以為這只不過是一種意思在句式上的兩種呈現，兩種說法在意義上其實有微妙的分別。試比較以下兩句：

(12) He gave some money to the beggar.

(13) He gave the beggar some money.

第一句中，some money 緊貼着動詞 gave，表示 money 就是動作 gave 的重點；第二句中，money 和 gave 中間隔了 the beggar，顯示 money 在句中的重要性較弱，反而誰接受了金錢更為重要。

有一首由 Barbara Streisand 和 Neil Diamond 主唱的老歌，內容講述一對男女感情轉淡，互相埋怨。你認為歌名應該是哪一個？

A　*You don't bring me flowers*

B　*You don't bring flowers to me*

原曲名為 You don't bring me flowers，對埋怨者來說，flowers 只是次要，me 才最重要。

42 文法是否一定合乎邏輯？

No 和 zero 也可以與複數名詞共用

我們一般會期望文法反映現實，舉例說，書架上明明一本書也沒有，英文沒理由會用到 book 的複數 books 吧？哪知文法歸文法，因為 book 是可數名詞，所以在一般情況下要說書架上沒有書，也要用複數名詞，故此應該是 There are no books on the shelf，等於 There aren't any books on the shelf。

　　可是，在特殊情況下，例如甲叮囑乙把椅子上的一本書找來，但乙找不到任何書本，那麼乙就可以用上 book 的單數形式，即 There is no book on the chair，因為甲和乙都是想着一本書。

　　同理，當一篇網上文章沒有人回應，我們一般可以說 No comments，但當某記者致電某高官，請他評論某事件，如果他不想回應，會說 No comment，雖然從文法上來講，No comments 也站得住腳。

Zero accidents! Zero 也是複數？

　　近年興起以 zero 去代替 no，那麼我們平常聽見的「零意外」，英文該是 zero accident 還是 zero accidents？答案是，因為 accident 是可數名詞，故此雖然 zero 意思上

是「沒有」，但按文法規定，像 There are no books 一樣，我們也要説 There are zero accidents，除非對話雙方都是想着一宗意外，但原來這宗意外不存在，才會説 There is no accident。

話説回來，zero 並非在任何情況下均可替代 no。試看看以下句子，讀起來是否有點奇怪？

(1) There are zero books on the shelf.

(2) There is zero money in my purse.

暫時所見，zero 只和 growth、accident、crime、loss 和 tolerance 等詞連用，並非任何情況下都可以使用 zero 代替 no。

以上説到，語文邏輯並不一定與事實吻合，且看以下對話：

Peter: 'You don't like Mary, do you?'

Paul. 'I do not *not* like her.'

Paul 的回答並不能以數學「負負得正」的原理解釋為 I like her。這種説法所表達的情感較為複雜，類似中文「我並非不喜歡她」的説法，即介乎喜歡與不喜歡之間。

再看看以下對話：

Peter: 'You don't like Mary, do you?'

Paul: 'Yes.'

Paul 的 Yes 是甚麼意思？是指 Peter 説得對，還是 Paul 其實是喜歡 Mary 的？

如果 Paul 是隨口説 Yes，他應該是附和 Peter 的説法；如果他其實是喜歡 Mary 的，便要費點唇舌，説明立場，不能有氣無力的説 Yes。如果他真的不喜歡 Mary，還是説 No, I don't 或 No, I don't like her 比較清楚了。

香港學生偶然弄不清楚，會這樣回答老師：

Teacher: 'You haven't done your homework?'

Student: '*Yes, I haven't.'

Teacher: 'You don't understand the question, do you?'

Student: '*Yes, I don't.'

有時候在快速的對話中，連母語是英語的人士也搞不清要說 Yes 還是 No。在法庭上，律師或有經驗的證人都會說 That's (not) correct，這便避免了說 Yes 或 No 所帶來的邏輯問題。

考考你

以下對話中，B 以平靜的語氣說 No，他究竟是否認同 A 的說法？

A: 'It doesn't snow in Hong Kong.'

B: 'No.'

答案：B 認同 A 的說法。B 也可以說 Yes，意思是「你說得正是」，即肯認。作為一個禮貌的回應，說 Yes 和 No 都可以。

43 別把祝福說成為慨嘆

怎樣用 wish 和 hope 表達祝福

EQ 題

要祝別人有一個愉快的假期，大家會
選用以下哪一句？

A I wish you a happy holiday.

B I wish you will have a happy holiday.

C I wish you to have a happy holiday.

D I hope you a happy holiday.

E I hope you will have a happy holiday.

F I hope you to have a happy holiday.

G Happy holiday.

偶爾收到學生的電郵或問候卡，上面寫的祝福句子包羅萬有，不過以下三句就讓我感到啼笑皆非：

(1) I wish you will have a happy vacation.

(2) I wish you enjoy your teaching.

(3) I wish you will have a merry Christmas.

他們本來想祝福我，卻錯用了「I wish ＋分句」的結構，令祝福變成了慨嘆。

我的學生之所以會寫錯祝福語，可能是以為 wish 和 hope 能隨意互換。不錯，我們可以說 I hope you will have a happy vacation，可是若要用 wish 表達祝福的話，wish 後面便要用名詞片語 (noun phrase)，例如 a happy vacation，即：

(4) I wish you a happy vacation.

(5) I wish you a merry Christmas.

如果 wish 後面不是名詞片語而是分句 (clause)，則整個句子立即變成表示惋惜和慨嘆，而非祝願，例如：

(6) I wish you were here.
（如果你在這裏，那有多好！）

(7) I wish I knew the answer.
（我也希望自己知道答案呢。）

(8) He wished he had not left her.
（他希望當初沒有離開她。）

因此祝福別人時，要不就用 I wish you a happy birthday 這類結構，要不就用「hope ＋分句」好了。

除了 wish 以外，英文還有幾個動詞，用在不同的句型中會有不同的意思，例如：

(9) I regret to inform you that I have to leave the school next month.

(10) I regret leaving school so early.

第 (9) 句中的 regret 接不定詞 (infinitive) to inform，句子的意思是「我對於下述事情感到遺憾」。第 (10) 句中的 regret 後接動名詞 (gerund) leaving，表示所說的事情早已發生，只是回想起來感到遺憾。

再舉一例：

(11) I didn't remember to lock the door.

(12) I don't remember seeing him before.

第 (11) 句指當時忘了鎖門，意思跟 I forgot to lock the door 類近；第 (12) 句則指回想起來似乎未曾見過他，並非忘了曾見過他。

又例如 I stopped to listen to her 和 I stopped listening to her，這兩句所表達的是兩個相反的行為！

除了 regret 和 remember，動詞 see、hear 和 feel 也有類似的用法：

A	B
(13) I saw her leave the office.	I saw her leaving the office.
(14) I heard someone climb into the house.	I heard someone climbing into the house.
(15) She felt herself walk into the house uncontrollably.	She felt herself blushing.

A 組句子在賓語後接不定詞，表示該動作已完成；B 組句子在賓語後接動名詞，表示動作仍在進行。以第 (13) 句為例，說 I saw her leave the office，表示句中的她已

離開了辦公室；若說 I saw her leaving the office，則表示她仍在辦公室，但正準備離開。其餘兩組句子的意思，也有類似的分別。

英文動詞用於不同句型，往往產生不同意思。對於這種用法上的差異，供學習者使用的詞典 (learner's dictionaries) 會清楚説明；相反，供母語人士使用的詞典，反而沒有這些資料呢！

知多一點點

英文有所謂的 verb pattern，指動詞與其他詞類或文法成分的搭配。牛津高階詞典 (*Oxford Advanced Learner's Dictionary*) 將最常用的二十種 verb pattern 都列出來了，是一個很方便的參考材料。

44 怎樣用英文説最宜居住的地方？

the best place to live 抑或 the best place to live in?

EQ 題

以下三組句子中，哪些句子是可以接受的？

A 1 These are the ten best places to live.

    2 These are the ten best places to live in.

B 3 These are the ten best cities to live.

    4 These are the ten best cities to live in.

C 5 Make sure you attend your personal belongings.

    6 Make sure you attend to your personal belongings.

    7 Make sure you don't leave your personal belongings unattended.

    8 Make sure you don't leave your personal belongings unattended to.

這個在維園的告示，你找到多少錯處？

　　康文署貼在維園的告示，本來是請遊人好好看管小童，但因為把 unsupervised 誤寫作 unsurprised，句子的意思變了「勿讓小童沒有驚喜」。父母若帶子女到維園，看來要不斷找點子逗他們了。除了上述的手民之誤外，告示中還有其他錯處，包括：

錯誤 (✗)	正確說法 (✓)
(1) No padding/climbing or feeding of bird/animals	No *paddling*, climbing or feeding of *birds*/animals
(2) No releasing fish/terrapin into the pool	No releasing fish/*terrapins* into the pool
(3) Prosecution will be taken.	Prosecution will be *made/brought/pursued/initiated*.

　　說回 Don't leave your children unsupervised，類似的句式有 Don't leave your personal belongings unattended，這一句是否有問題？Unattended 後面是否漏了介詞 to？

　　根據英文文法，部分動詞後面要接介詞，例如 reply：

　　(4) Please reply me.　　(✗)

　　(5) Please reply *to* me. (✓)

另一個容易錯用的單詞是 enrol，如果要說報讀某課程，enrol 後面要接介詞 on：

(6) I enrolled the first-aid course.　　(✗)

(7) I enrolled *on* the first-aid course. (✓)

留意 enrol 後面也可不用介詞，但意思會變成「錄取」，例如 The first-aid course has enrolled 20 students，解作「這門急救課程錄取了 20 名學生」。

動詞 attend 指「注意」或「處理」時，也不能略去 to：

(8) Doctor Lee had to attend to many patients at the same time.

(9) I have several things to attend to.

上述與動詞共用的介詞，在另一個句式下可否省去？試比較：

(10a)　Mr Wong is the person he replied.

(10b)　Mr Wong is the person he replied to.

(11a)　This is the course I have enrolled.

(11b)　This is the course I have enrolled on.

(12a)　These are the patients Doctor Lee attended.

(12b)　These are the patients Doctor Lee attended to.

以上三組的 (a) 句都有問題。

如果要說 These are the patients Doctor Lee attended to，而當 attend 變為形容詞 unattended 時，是否也要和 to 共用？

(13a)　Don't leave your personal belongings unattended.

(13b)　Don't leave your personal belongings unattended to.

文法上 Don't leave your personal belongings unattended to 這句子正確無誤，但在實際使用中，句末的 to 常會略去。(13a) 和 (13b) 的說法都沒有問題。

請大家再看以下兩句：

(14a)　He is looking for the best place to live.

(14b)　He is looking for the best place to live in.

既然我們說 to live in a place 而非 to live a place，理論上 (14b) 才算正確，可是在日常生活中，(14a) 會更為普遍。

那麼，將 place 改為 city 又如何？

(15a)　Seattle is the best city to live.

(15b)　Seattle is the best city to live in.

一旦將 place 改為 city，句末的介詞 in 便不能省略。即 (15a) 有問題。

要掌握這種慣用法，文法規條幫不上忙，只能靠平日多聽多看，及提高自己對語言的敏感度，才能好好掌握。

請小心照顧子女
Do not leave your children unsupervised

請勿嬉水
No paddling

請勿把魚／龜放進模型船池
No releasing of fish and terrapin into the model boat pool

嚴禁擺賣　違例者會被檢控
No hawking
Offender will be prosecuted

說回維園的告示。後來告示換上了這個版本，這一次是否正確無誤？

告示仍然有錯誤：terrapin 應改作 terrapins，offender 應改作 offenders。

考考你

下面兩句中遺漏了甚麼介詞？

A　Please apply the scholarship as soon as you can.

B　Our course caters the needs of young children.

答案：A　Please apply *for* the scholarship as soon as you can.
　　　B　Our course caters *to/for* the needs of young children.

45 擾人的關係分句

要學懂分析但仍要靠多聽多讀

英文句子中只要有名詞,便可以加上關係分句 (relative clause)。就是這個特性,讓英文句子理論上可以無限擴展。由於中文沒有類似的結構,而關係分句又千變萬化,要純熟掌握關係分句,確實不易,以下便是常見的錯誤:

(1) She likes the handbag which I bought it for her.　　(✗)

為甚麼關係分句會特別難掌握?請大家看看以下兩個句子:

(2) That's the *strange* person.

(3) That's the person *who has been staring at you*.

兩個句子同是形容 person,第 (2) 句的形容詞 strange 放在 person 前面;第 (3) 句的關係分句 who has been staring at you,則放在 person 後面。再請大家試用中文翻譯這兩個句子,看看有甚麼發現?不錯,第 (3) 句的中譯是「那就是一直盯着你的人」,修飾語「一直盯着你」的位置跟英文正好相反!

此外,如果要修飾的名詞,在關係分句中扮演賓語 (object) 的角色,那麼在關係分句中要不要採用代名詞 (pronoun),會容易造成錯誤:

(4) She likes the handbag which I bought it for her.　　(✗)

(5) She likes the handbag which I bought for her.　　(✓)

(6) Those are the children whom I played with them last Sunday.　　(✗)

(7) Those are the children whom I played with last Sunday.　　(✓)

關係代名詞甚麼時候可省去,甚麼時候不可?看看以下的句子,哪些可略去關係代名詞 (relative pronoun)?

(8) That's the person *who* has been staring at you.

(9) She likes the handbag *which* I bought for her.

(10) Those are the children *whom* I played with last Sunday.

(11) Do you like the handbag *which* I bought for you?

(12) Do you like the handbag *that* I bought for you?

(13) Those are the people *that* have worked tirelessly behind the project.

(14) Those are the people *who* have worked tirelessly behind the project.

(15) Those are the people *whom* I mentioned to you yesterday.

(16) Those are the people *whom* I talked to this morning.

(17) Those are the people to *whom* I talked this morning.

以上的句 (9)、(10)、(11)、(12)、(15)、(16) 中的關係代名詞都可以略去，但背後的法則是甚麼？

以上的例句還帶出其他的問題，例如：

- 以 (11) 和 (12) 來說，用 which 或 that 是否全無分別？

- 以 (13) 和 (14) 來說，that 和 who 之間應如何取捨？

- 以 (15) 來說，whom 可否以 who 取代？

- 以 (16) 和 (17) 來說，哪個說法較為常見？

還有，下面 (18) 和 (19) 有分別嗎？

(18) That's the city in which I grew up.

(19) That's the city where I grew up.

至於下面的 which is quite unimaginable，又應怎樣分析？

(20) I have bought her over ten handbags this year, *which is quite unimaginable.*

你說累不累人？我還未說到限定性關係分句 (defining relative clause) 和非限定性關係分句 (non-defining relative clause) 的分別呢！

英語課程和教科書都會用大量篇幅，並輔以大量練習，去解釋和教授關係分句，有時候真的把學生弄得頭昏腦漲。我認為，應引導學生留意在真實文章中，作者如何使用關係分句，並找出其結構，這也是很重要的。

46 小心歧義句

文法和我們開的玩笑

按一般人的印象，英文文法較中文文法嚴謹，例如英文句子通常不能略去主語，動詞的形態不能馬虎，名詞要分辨是可數還是不可數等等。因為有這種種規條，於是人們以為英文句子一定不會出現歧義，但其實並不一定。語言學上的經典例子是 The chicken is ready to eat，究竟是誰吃誰？

上一頁中的 My sister didn't become a nurse because of the pay，可以指：

(1) My sister didn't become a nurse. This was because of the pay.

(2) My sister became a nurse, but not because of the pay.

第 (1) 句暗示護士的工資不理想，第 (2) 句則是指工資並非主要考慮因素。

這些容易產生歧義的句子，多為否定句。請看看以下對話：

A: 'I'm going to quit my job soon.'

B: 'You can't be serious.'

到底 B 的回應是責怪 A 看待工作不夠嚴肅，還是叮囑 A 不要太認真？答案是兩者皆不是。原來 B 認為 A 只不過是隨便說說而已。

再分析另一個包含 cannot 的例子：

(3) The importance of hard work cannot be over-emphasized.

到底說話者認為勤奮工作是否重要？

按字面分析，這句話的意思該是「勤奮工作不應被過分強調」，可實際解釋卻是「勤奮工作非常重要，重要到無論我們怎樣強調都不嫌過」。

口語中有 I can't/couldn't agree more，為甚麼這句話的意思是「我完全同意」，而不是「我只是有限度地同意」？這個句子的分析方法和上面一樣：我是那麼的同意，以致無論怎樣，都不能比現時更同意。一位臉書朋友便經常打趣道：「我不能夠同意得更多了。」

從而我們便不難解釋為甚麼在以下對話中，Susan 不是指她不能不關心，而是指她才不會理會呢！

Mary: 'Helen has been talking behind your back.'

Susan: 'Well, I couldn't care less.'

口語中有 You can say that again 的説法。請看以下對話：

John: 'The guy is a complete idiot.'

Peter: 'You can say that again.'

留意 Peter 並不是真的請 John 再説一遍，Peter 的意思其實是「那還用説嗎？」，這是習用説法，不能取其字面意思。

英語文法的某些特性，也會引致歧義。下面三句有甚麼歧義？歧義來自甚麼？

(4) Visiting professors can be boring.

(5) The old men and women sat in the park.

(6) The policeman stopped the man with a gun.

句 (4) 的 visiting 可以是形容詞，visiting professors 是客座教授；visiting 也可以是動名詞 (gerund)，visiting professors 就是指探訪教授這行動。句 (5) 的 women 既可以為 old 所修飾，即 the old women，也可以是獨立存在，即 the women。句 (6) 的 with a gun，可以指 the man with a gun，也可以是狀語 (adverbial)，指出 The policeman stopped the man 的方法。

　　要避免說了有歧義的句子而不自知，靠的還是敏銳的語言覺識 (language awareness)。

47 性別歧視在英文

性別公平意識如何影響文法？

以下哪些句子是可接受的？

(1) Everyone likes Jane, doesn't he?

(2) Everyone likes Jane, doesn't he or she?

(3) Everyone likes Jane, don't they?

(4) Everything is fine, isn't it?

(5) Everything is fine, aren't they?

在英文中，當主句的主語是 Everyone 或 Everybody 時，附加疑問句 (question tag) 的代名詞是複數的 they，而不是單數的 he，例如 Everybody likes Jane, don't they?，理據可以是 Everyone 指所有人，意思上是複數，但有趣的是主語如果是 Everything，則附加疑問句的代名詞是單數的 it，例如 Everything is fine, isn't it?，而不是 *Everything is fine, aren't they?，可見這除了是 Everybody 的意思外，還是一個語言與性別的課題。

你會否刻意避免使用下列的詞語？

fireman, postman, policeman, chairman, businessman, salesman, layman, mankind, man-made, to man a booth, headmaster/headmistress, waiter/waitress, steward/stewardess

近年西方國家提倡性別公平 (gender-fair) 的語言運用，像 fireman、postman 一類的詞語，已經近乎「禁用」，而改為 fire fighter、police officer、chairperson、businessperson、salesperson 和 layperson。至於一些同時存在男性詞和女性詞的詞彙，他們也提倡不用，例如以 principal 代替 headmaster 和 headmistress，以 server 代替 waiter 和 waitress，以 flight attendant 和 cabin crew 代替 air host/steward 和 air hostess/stewardess。

但有時候要想出一個妥貼的無性別詞，也不一定容易，policeman 和 policewoman 還可以用 police officer 代替，但如果你看見以下三個詞，你會想起甚麼：

(6) postal worker

(7) mail deliverer

(8) letter carrier

這三個詞都有人提倡用以取代 postman，但它們能完全表達 postman 的意思嗎？Postal worker 可泛指郵務職員，而 mail deliverer、letter carrier 和 messenger 三者又有何分別？Messenger 和 postman 在意思上卻又不完全一樣啊！

那麼，可否保留 postman 一詞？而如果是女郵差的話，稱其為 female postman，像 male nurse 一樣，可以嗎？

西方國家不少學術和專業組織都會發出指引，指示正確的性別公平用語。美國最大的英語教師組織是 National Council of Teachers of English (NCTE)，NCTE 認為不應使用 female postman 和 male nurse 這樣有性別標籤的職業詞，連 a woman doctor 都應該改為 a doctor who is a woman！

性別公平語言還涉及文法，尤其是各種一致關係 (agreement)。以前 A manager should be aware of the morale of his staff，沒人會覺得 his staff 有問題，但自從人們對性別公平語言意識提高，便開始改說 A manager should be aware of the morale of his or her staff，但這類句子寫下來累贅，說出來又不順口，於是現時有人用 their 去取代 his or her，即 A manager should be aware of the morale of their staff，但你又是否接受用複數的 their 去配合單數的 a manager？

NCTE 提出的辦法是一律採用複數主語，即說 Managers should be aware of the morale of their staffs，但從傳意效果來說，單數主語和複數主語始終是有分別的。試比較：

(9) During the interview, each candidate is given two minutes to introduce himself or herself.

(10) During the interview, candidates are each given two minutes to introduce themselves.

句 (10) 以複數名詞 candidates 代替 each candidate，雖避去說 his，或 his or her，但感覺便不及 each candidate 那麼精準。

說到這裏，日漸流行又不跟傳統文法的 Each candidate is given two minutes to introduce themselves，也是不錯的解決辦法啊！

考考你

以下 NCTE 建議的修改，你是否同意？

1 Does each student have his book?
   → Does each student have their book?

2 Maria is a career woman.
   → Maria is a professional.

3 The ladies on the committee all supported the bill.
   → The women on the committee all supported the bill.

資料來源：http://www.ncte.org/positions/statements/genderfairuseoflang

48 情態動詞的雙重意義

為何有人說 will 不表示 future tense？

開不到？不准開？

這家在曼谷 MBK 商場內的小店，賣的是手機套，貨品都包裝在膠袋裏。顯然有不少人試而不買，店主唯有下令不准開啟、不准試用，而並非說這些膠袋是打不開的。

然而在文法上，情態動詞 (modal verb) can 和 can't 的確又具有兩種意義。在以下的對話中，父親正是玩弄 can 的雙重意義：

Child: 'Can I watch television?'

Father: 'You can, but you may not.'

Can 有兩層意義，一是和能力有關，意思類似 able to；二是和准許有關，類似 allowed to。小孩問的是父親是否准許他看電視，但父親說 You can，取其能力的意思去調侃小孩，然後改用 may not 去拒絕請求。

情態動詞有 can、may、must、will 和 shall。這些詞之所以難掌握，在於它們似乎有很多不同意思；而情態動詞的過去形式 (past form)，即 could、might、would、should 又不一定和過去有關。先說意義，以下句子中的情態動詞應怎樣理解？

(1) You may leave now.

(2) It may rain tomorrow.

(3) He can speak Japanese fluently.

(4) That can't be true.

(5) That woman must be quite rich.

(6) The students must do it again.

(7) I won't help him.

(8) They will get married soon.

(9) If you take a taxi, you should be there in 10 minutes.

(10) He should keep quiet.

英語課程介紹情態動詞時，會傾向集中介紹上面句
(1)、(2)、(3)、(6)、(8) 和 (10) 的基本意思，即：

May 指准許、可能　　You may leave now.

It may rain tomorrow.

Can 指能力　　　　　He can speak Japanese fluently.

Must 指規定　　　　　The students must do it again.

Will 指計劃、預測　　They will get married soon.

Should 指行為準則　　He should keep quiet.

但很明顯，That can't be true 和能力無關；That
woman must be quite rich 不是我們所能控制；You should
be there in 10 minutes 也不表示對方應否做某件事情。

情態動詞有多種用法，但原來最後都可歸納為兩類
意義。第一類是認知情態 (epistemic modality)，即情態動
詞用來顯示我們對事物的認知，例如：

(11) (He has stayed in Japan for four years.) He can speak
Japanese fluently.

(12) (That woman owns six houses.) She must be quite rich.

(13) (Look at the dark clouds.) It may rain tomorrow.

(14) (They have been together for a few years.) They will
get married soon.

(15) (The taxi is quick.) You should be there in 10 minutes.

第二類是道義情態 (deontic modality)，即情態動詞用
來顯示立場與態度，例如：

(16) (I can see that you have finished all your work.) You
may leave now.

(17) (I am very familiar with those things.) That can't be true.

(18) (I think the students have done their homework
carelessly.) They must do it again.

(19) (He has been unkind to me.) I won't help him.

(20) (I think he has been talking too much.) He should keep quiet.

由於情態動詞有這兩類意思，有時候會出現歧義：

(21) Your friend may not leave. (你的朋友也許不走了。／你的朋友不得離開。)

(22) You must have a lot of money. (你一定要有很多錢，才能……。／你這樣豪爽，你一定是很有錢了！)

情態動詞的確不易掌握，但如能運用自如，確能幫助我們把更複雜的情意表達出來。

49 怎樣提示乘客在哪側下車

如何決定甚麼做句子的主語？

香港港鐵廣播：

Doors will open on the left.

誰對誰錯？

東京地鐵廣播：

The doors on the left
side will open.

在文法上，Doors will open on the left 和 The doors on the left side will open 都沒有問題，但為甚麼聽起來意思上總是有點分別？哪種說法較合邏輯？我們先以「主語＋謂語」(subject + predicate) 的分析句子方法，試試是否能看出端倪。在這分析法下，主語就是我們一般認識的主語，謂語就是句子的其餘部分。

主語	謂語
(1) Doors	will open on the left.
(2) The doors on the left side	will open.

也許你已經有一些頭緒，(1) 和 (2) 有不同的主語和謂語。現在我們再想想這廣播出現的場合和廣播的意圖。

列車抵達車站時，有時候月台在左，有時候在右，廣播的目的，就是預先提示乘客應該在哪一邊下車，讓他們有所準備。在這個背景下，大家再重看 (1) 和 (2)，會否覺得 (1) 較為妥當？

從句子的資訊結構 (information structure) 來看，一般無標記（unmarked，即典型形式）句子可分析為「主題＋評論」(topic + comment)，和「主語＋謂語」句型配合。即：

主題	評論
(1) Doors	will open on the left.
(2) The doors on the left side	will open.

主題顯示這句子說的是關於甚麼事情，評論就是就着這主題要說的內容。句 (2) 像在說：「我現在說說左邊的車門，這車門將會打開啊」。

但乘客要知道的，不是這左側的車門會做甚麼，他們要知道的是車門開在左邊還是右邊；句 (2) 文法正確，但重點錯置。

另外，英文還傾向把主要要表達的資訊放在句子後端，即「重心在尾」(end weight)，乘客要知道的是左或右，句 (1) 把 on the left 放在後端，這正好符合了「重心在尾」的原則。

說到這裏，大家也許明白寫作的指引為甚麼告誡我們不要濫用被動式 (passive voice)。試用「主題＋評論」方法去分析下面的口號 (slogan)：

主題	評論
(3) Our effort	is made to achieve a cleaner harbour for the future of Hong Kong.

這口號要告訴人的，是他們在做甚麼，用 We 作為句子的主題便好了，在無緣無故下用 Our effort 作主題，不易引起注意，兼且謂語是被動式，好像 Our effort「被發生」了一些事情，這並非他們真正要說的。

除了句子分析,「主題＋評論」這概念也可應用於某些語言的特性,例如中文和日文都是「主題顯著」(topic-prominent) 語言 (註)。圖中是我在日本碰到的文法錯誤,大家也許見怪不怪,你能看出來嗎?

註:Li, Charles N.; Thompson, Sandra A (1976). Subject and Topic: A New Typology of Language. In Charles N. Li. *Subject and Topic*. New York: Academic Press, page 475.

知多一點點

七零年代初由學者 Michael Halliday 帶動的系統功能語法 (systemic functional grammar),開啟了另一個今天舉足輕重的分析語文的方法,就是分析句子的「主題＋述位」(theme + rheme),大大豐富了傳統文法分析。

50 説 Mind the gap between train and platform 妥當嗎？

語境重於一切

香港港鐵廣播：

Please mind the gap
between the train and
the platform.

誰對誰錯？

曼谷捷運廣播：

Please mind the gap
between train and
platform.

中文沒有冠詞 (article)，所以我們使用英語時常見的一個錯誤，就是在單數的可數名詞前忘記使用冠詞。但是在一些情況下，冠詞的確是可以省去的。

例如我們熟悉的 They go to school by bus，不需要說 by a bus 或 by the bus，類似的例子有 by car、by train、by ship、by taxi 和 on foot，小學時老師也許把它們當為指交通工具時的特定說法，學生只要加以背熟便可以了。但是英文冠詞的運用，全然是基於背後的思維。

當我們說 go to school by bus 時，bus 已經不代表有形的實物，我們亦不是想着某一輛巴士，bus 只是一個意念，故此不需要說 a bus (一輛巴士) 或 the bus (某輛巴士)。同理，我們說 by car、by train、by ship、by taxi 和 on foot 時都不用冠詞 (zero article)。如果再看看 go to school by bus，我們會發現 school 前也沒有冠詞，道理也一樣，school 在這裏是一個意念，故此我們也說 go to university 和 go to college。

在眾多常用片語中，如 in bed、go to church、taken to hospital、have lunch、in prison、at work、in town 等，名詞前面都不用冠詞，也是同一道理。

除了上述情況外，在一些語境下，如果所指的人和物是對話雙方共同知悉的，即是說已經完全沒有需要用 the 去表明所指的時候，也無須使用冠詞。中學時很喜歡流行歌手 Cat Stevens 的一首歌，歌名是 *Father and Son*，內容就是典型的父子之間的關係，歌名不是 *A/The Father and a/the Son*。類似 father and son 的例子還有 husband and wife、teacher and student。例如一段文章描述兩夫婦的遭遇，文章的中、後段便大有可能出現 both husband and wife … 的寫法。這用法在說明書的指示和烹飪書中尤其常見，很多時所有的冠詞都會省去。

港鐵的月台廣播有 Please mind the gap between the train and the platform，這裏 the gap and the platform 的 the，乃指某特定的 train 和 platform，即停在那裏的列車，和乘客身處的月台；但曼谷捷運的廣播卻是 Please mind the gap between train and platform，這廣播只說 train 和 platform，有問題嗎？

在架空月台中，如果設計廣播的人認為，train 和 platform 是身處那地方的人必然會明白所指的是甚麼，那麼廣播中直接說 the gap between train and platform，絕無問題。當然，說 the gap between the train and the platform 亦沒錯。

故此，使用冠詞與否，並非機械式的規條，而是反映了背後的思維；認識到這一點，我們更能體驗到文法的樂趣呢！

財經界有一常用語：Cash is king，說的是現金的重要性，king 是可數名詞 (countable noun)，但為甚麼是 king，而不是 a king 或 the king？相信大家都可以看出原因了。

知多一點點

除了 go to school 和 go to university，我們也可說 go to kindergarten。至於 play group（或 playgroup），也可說 go to playgroup 或 attend playgroup，但 tutorial centre 在概念上不是教育歷程的必然階段，故此一般會說 attend tutorial centres/classes。

有關語言覺識的閱讀書目

Andrews, S. (2007a). Teacher language awareness [electronic resource]. Cambridge: Cambridge University Press.

Ardnt, V., Harvey, P., & Nuttall, J. (2000). *Alive to language: Perspectives on language awareness for English language teachers.* Cambridge: Cambridge University Press.

Berry, R. (2015). Grammar myths. *Language Awareness, 24*(1), 15–37.

Biber, D., Johansson, S., Leech, G., Conrad, S., & Finegan, Ed. (1999). *Longman grammar of spoken and written English.* Harlow: Longman.

Bolitho, R., & Tomlinson, B. (1995). *Discover English : A language awareness workbook* (New ed.). Oxford: Heinemann.

Carter, R. (1995). How aware should language aware teachers and learners be? In D. Nunan, R. Berry, & V. Berry (Eds.), *Language awareness in language education* (pp. 1–15). Hong Kong: Department of Curriculum Studies, The University of Hong Kong.

Carter, R. (2003). Key concepts in ELT: Language awareness. *ELT Journal, 57*(1), 64–65.

Carter, R., & McCarthy, M. (1994). Grammar and the spoken language. *Applied Linguistics, 16*(2), 141–158.

Carter, R., & McCarthy, M. (2006). *Cambridge grammar of English: A comprehensive guide to spoken and written English grammar and usage.* Cambridge: Cambridge University Press.

Doughty, C., & Varela, E. (1998). Communicative focus on form. In C. Doughty & J. Williams (Eds.), *Focus on form in classroom second language acquisition* (pp. 114–138). Cambridge: Cambridge University Press.

Doughty, C., & Williams, J. (Eds.). (1998). *Focus on form in classroom second language acquisition.* Cambridge: Cambridge University Press.

Fontaine, L. (2013). *Analysing English grammar.* Cambridge: Cambridge University Press.

Harley, B. (1998). The role of focus-on-form tasks in promoting child L2 acquisition. In C. Doughty & J. Williams (Eds.), *Focus on form in classroom second language acquisition* (pp. 156–174). Cambridge: Cambridge University Press.

Halliday, M.A.K. (2004). *An introduction to functional grammar* (3rd ed.). London: Arnold.

Hawkins, E. W. (1987). *Awareness of language: An introduction* (rev. ed.). Cambridge: Cambridge University Press.

Kennedy, S. (2012). Exploring the relationship between language awareness and second language use. *TESOL Quarterly, 46*(2), 398–408.

Larsen-Freeman, D. (2004). *Teaching language: From grammar to grammaring*. Boston: Thomson/Heinle.

Liamkina, O., & Ryshina-Pankova, M. (2012). Grammar dilemma: Teaching grammar as a resource for making meaning. *Modern Language Journal, 96*(2), 270–289.

Lightbown, P. M. (1998). The importance of timing in focus on form. In C. Doughty & J. Williams (Eds.), *Focus on form in classroom second language acquisition* (pp. 177–196). Cambridge: Cambridge University Press.

Lightbown, P. M., & Spada, N. (2013). *How languages are learned* (4th ed.). Oxford: Oxford University Press.

Liu, D. (2011). Making grammar instruction more empowering: An exploratory case study of corpus use in the learning/teaching of grammar. *Research in the Teaching of English, 45*(4), 353–377.

Long, M. H., & Robinson, P. (1998). Focus on form: Theory, research, and practice. In C. Doughty & J. Williams (Eds.), *Focus on form in classroom second language acquisition* (pp. 15–41). Cambridge: Cambridge University Press.

McBride-Chang, C., Cheung, H., Chow, B. W. Y., Chow, C. S. L., & Choi, L. (2006). Metalinguistic skills and vocabulary knowledge in Chinese (L1) and English (L2). *Reading and Writing: An Interdisciplinary Journal, 19*(7), 695–716.

Muñoz, C. (2013). Exploring young learners' foreign language learning awareness. *Language Awareness, 23*(1–2), 24–40.

Nunan, D., Berry, R., & Berry, V. (Eds.). (1995). *Language awareness in language education*. Department of Curriculum Studies, The University of Hong Kong.

Radwan, A. A. (2005). The effectiveness of explicit attention to form in language learning. *System: An International Journal of Educational Technology and Applied Linguistics, 33*(1), 69–87.

Roberts, A. D. (2011). *The role of metalinguistic awareness in the effective teaching of foreign languages*. Bern, Switzerland: Peter Lang.

Ruan, Z. (2013). Metacognitive awareness of EFL student writers in a Chinese ELT context. *Language Awareness, 23*(1–2), 76–91.

Sze, P., & Fung, F.Y.L. (2014). Enhancing learners' metalinguistic awareness of language form: The use of eTutor resources. *Assessment and Learning, Issue 3*, 79–96.

Thompson, G. (2013). *Introducing functional grammar* (3rd ed.). London: Routledge.

Thornbury, S. (1997). *About language: Tasks for teachers of English*. Cambridge: Cambridge University Press.

Thornbury, S. (2001). *Uncovering grammar*. Oxford : Macmillan Heinemann.

Tuzel, A. E. B., & Akcan, S. (2009). Raising the language awareness of pre-service English Teachers in an EFL Context. *European Journal of Teacher Education, 32*(3), 271–287.

Watson, A. M. (2013). Conceptualisations of 'grammar teaching': L1 English teachers' beliefs about teaching grammar for writing. *Language Awareness, 24*(1), 1–14.

Williams, J., & Evans, J. (1998). What kind of focus and on which forms? In C. Doughty & J. Williams (Eds.), *Focus on form in classroom second language acquisition* (pp. 139–155). Cambridge: Cambridge University Press.

Xu, H., & Lyster, R. (2014). Differential effects of explicit form-focused instruction on morphosyntactic development. *Language Awareness, 23*(1–2), 107–122.

林沛理 (2011)。《英文玩家》(第三版)。香港：天窗出版。

林沛理 (2014)。《英文智商》。香港：天窗出版。

唐明、陳國榮 (2014)。《英語‧人生》。香港：牛津大學出版社。

歐陽偉豪、施敏文 (2011)。《中英大不同：語法解密》。香港：青桐社。

歐陽偉豪、施敏文 (2012)。《中英大不同 2：錯了就嘩爆的語法問題》。香港：青桐社。